2025

ULTIMATE FOOTBALL HEROES

First published by Dino Books in 2024,
an imprint of Bonnier Books UK,
4th Floor, Victoria House, Bloomsbury Square, London WC1B 4DA
Owned by Bonnier Books,
Sveavägen 56, Stockholm, Sweden

X @UFHbooks
www.heroesfootball.com
www.bonnierbooks.co.uk

Irish Edition ISBN: 978 1 78946 874 8
Paperback ISBN: 978 1 78946 752 9
E-book ISBN: 978 1 78946 813 7

Written by Matt Oldfield, Emily Stead, Seth Burkett and John Murray
Edited by Emil Fortune
Design by Alessandro Susin
Cover illustrations by Dan Leydon
Production by Natalie Tang

British Library cataloguing-in-publication data:
A catalogue record for this book is available from the British Library.

Printed and bound in Great Britain by Clays Ltd, Elcograf S.p.A.

3 5 7 9 10 8 6 4 2

MIX
Paper | Supporting responsible forestry
FSC® C018072

2025
ULTIMATE FOOTBALL HEROES

Matt Oldfield

Emily Stead

Seth Burkett

John Murray

DINO

INTRODUCTION

Welcome to *Ultimate Football Heroes 2025* – a new annual round-up of the most exciting stories from a thrilling season of the beautiful game!

Matt Oldfield and Emily Stead recap rollercoaster title races in the English Premier League and Women's Super League, featuring Liverpool, Arsenal, Manchester City and Chelsea.

John Murray brings you all the European club cup glory, plus Euro 2024 and the best of the action from the big leagues in France, Germany, Spain, Italy and Scotland.

And Seth Burkett picks the best goals, games, players, performances and much, much more from around the world of football.

You can also test your knowledge with a giant-sized quiz, hunt for football heroes in our fiendish word-search and crack the clues in a football themed crossword, among other activities.

The players are ready … the fans are raring to go … let's blow the whistle on *Ultimate Football Heroes 2025!*

MEET THE AUTHORS

Matt Oldfield is a children's author focusing on the wonderful world of football. His other books include *Unbelievable Football* (winner of the 2020 Children's Sports Book of the Year) and the *Johnny Ball: Football Genius* series. In association with his writing, Matt also delivers writing workshops in schools.

Seth Burkett is an author, ghostwriter and former professional footballer. Having played in Brazil and Sri Lanka, Seth now dedicates his time to writing and speaking in schools. He has published 16 books, including *Tekkers* and *The Football GOAT* series.

Emily Stead has loved writing for children ever since she was a child herself! Working as a children's writer and editor, she has created books about some of football's biggest stars, teams and tournaments for many a season. When she's not writing, you can probably find her watching from the sidelines at her youngest son's matches or attempting to play the beautiful game herself in Yorkshire.

John Murray has written and edited books on a wide range of sports, from football and fencing to tennis and Test cricket. He is the content director at Touchline.

TABLE OF CONTENTS

ENGLISH PREMIER LEAGUE

PART 1

DECLAN RICE GUNNING FOR GLORY

At the end of the 2022–23 football season, it was decision time for Declan. He was delighted to be leaving his beloved West Ham on a high, after leading the club to the UEFA Europa Conference League title, their first major trophy in forty-three years, but where next for England's number one defensive midfielder?

Chelsea? No – while Declan still loved his boyhood club, he didn't want to go back there.

Bayern Munich? No – in the end he proved too expensive for the German giants.

Manchester City? No – although he loved the idea of playing for the English and European Champions, they already had Rodri, the best defensive midfielder in the world, as well as Declan's England teammate Kalvin Phillips.

Manchester United? The Red Devils had Casemiro for now, but they felt Declan would be the perfect long-term replacement. Plus, his best friend Mason Mount had just signed for the club . . .

Liverpool? The Reds were looking to rebuild their midfield and they believed Declan was the right man for the job . . .

Arsenal? The Gunners already had Thomas Partey and Jorginho, but after finishing second in the Premier League behind Manchester City, manager Mikel Arteta wanted to upgrade his midfield, and he saw Declan as the missing piece of the title-winning puzzle. Plus, Declan would get to stay living in London . . .

Hmmm, so many interesting options, but which one would he choose? On 15 July, Declan announced his big decision to the world at last. He was signing for . . .

Arsenal!

'New beginnings,' he wrote on social media, alongside a first photo of him in the famous red and white kit. 'COYG (Come on You Gunners).'

The club had paid a record fee of £105 million for him, making Declan the new most expensive English player ever! Wow, that was a lot of money and a lot of pressure, but he was determined to make a difference and prove that he was worth every penny.

Declan made his competitive debut for his new club in the Community Shield, where the Gunners fought back from 1–0 down to beat Manchester City on penalties. Hurray, glory already!

'First trophy for The Arsenal!' Declan posted happily. Now, he couldn't wait for the new Premier League campaign to kick off.

For their opening game of the 2023–24 season, at home against Nottingham Forest, Arteta named a very attacking line-up: a front three of Gabriel Martinelli, Eddie Nketiah and Bukayo Saka, plus Kai Havertz and Martin Ødegaard in midfield. Really, wasn't that a bit risky? No, because Arsenal now had Declan in defensive midfield, to sit deep, read the game, and deal with any danger.

Tackles,

headers,

blocks,

interceptions,

recovery runs . . .

Declan did them all, calmly and confidently, helping his team to a 2–1 victory against Forest, and then a 1–0 win away at Crystal Palace.

'Come onnnnnnn!' Declan roared, punching the air with passion. Arsenal were off to a strong start, and there was plenty more to come, especially from their new record signing. Because Declan was a midfielder who could do a lot more than just defend. He had an excellent range of passing, loved to burst forward and dribble with the ball, and had a powerful strike too . . .

Deep in injury time, Arsenal were heading for a disappointing draw at home against Manchester United, but Declan was still desperate to get the win. So as Bukayo curled in one last corner, he snuck in unmarked at the back post, chested the ball down, and then smashed a shot past the keeper. *2–1!*

Goooooooooooooooooooooooooooooaaaaaaaaaaaaaaaaaaaaallllllllllllllllllllllllllllllllllllllll!!!!!!!!!!!!!!!!

Yesssssssss, what a feeling! While the supporters

went wild all around the Emirates Stadium, Declan slid towards the corner flag on his knees, followed by all of his ecstatic teammates.

'You hero!' Gabriel Magalhães shouted, jumping up on Declan's back, right in front of the celebrating fans.

Big performances in the biggest games – that's what the club had paid all that money for. A few weeks later, Declan was Arsenal's man of the match again, but this time back in his usual defensive midfield role. Against their big title rivals Manchester City, Arteta didn't want him bursting forward to try and score more goals; no, his job was to sit deep alongside Jorginho, win the ball back for his team, and keep things calm and simple.

Yes, Boss! Declan ran and ran all match long,

winning tackles,

making interceptions,

and playing lots of accurate passes. He even cleared a shot from Joško Gvardiol off his own goal line!

'You hero!' Gabriel Magalhães cried out again.

With ten minutes left, the score was still 0–0. A draw against City would be a decent result for Arsenal, especially this early in the season, but Declan and his teammates were desperate to grab all three points. Kai chested the ball down in the box and laid it back to Gabriel Martinelli, whose shot deflected off a defender and into the bottom corner. *1–0!*

'Come onnnnnnnn!' Declan cheered with joy and relief and ran over to join in the team celebrations. What an important win it might prove to be!

Arsenal weren't yet playing the same kind of dynamic, attacking football that they had the previous season, but they certainly looked more solid at the back. Gabriel Magalhães and William Saliba had formed the best centre-back partnership in the Premier League, and in front of them, they now had Declan, one of the best defensive midfielders in the world. No wonder the Gunners were keeping more clean sheets!

With ten games played, Arsenal sat tied with City in second place, just two points behind their North London rivals Tottenham. Not bad – but they would definitely need to improve if they were going to lift the Premier League title this time. The good news for the Gunners was that they were still unbeaten. The not quite so good news was that they had already drawn three matches that they really should have won:

2–2 at home against Fulham, who had scored an equaliser in the eighty-seventh minute . . .

2–2 at home in the North London derby against Tottenham, where Arsenal went 1–0 and then 2–0 up . . .

. . . and finally, 2–2 away at Chelsea. From 2–0 down, Declan had done his best to inspire his team to victory again with a fantastic strike from thirty yards, but in the end, Arsenal had to settle for one point instead of three. Never mind, there were still many more matches to play . . .

MO SALAH
SAME OLD SUPERSTAR

Meanwhile over at Liverpool, it felt like the end of a golden era. After a trophyless 2022–23 season, the club had said an emotional goodbye to six of their most experienced players:

Roberto Firmino,
Alex Oxlade-Chamberlain,
Naby Keïta,
James Milner,
Jordan Henderson,
and Fabinho.

So many incredible characters, and so many happy memories of winning the UEFA Champions League and the Premier League together!

But what about Mo? He was thirty-one years old now, and after seeing lots of his old teammates move on, would he decide to leave too? Saudi Arabian club Al-Ittihad made a late £150 million offer to sign him, but despite the massive fee, Liverpool said no. Their most famous superstar was absolutely not for sale! They needed Mo to stay; he was one of their senior leaders now, along with Alisson and Virgil van Dijk, and he was also still the team's most lethal attacker.

Over the last few years, the club had added new, younger forwards like Diogo Jota, Luis Díaz, Darwin Núñez, and Cody Gakpo, but for all their speed and skill, none of them could score as many as Mo, year after year. 'The Egyptian King' had finished with at least nineteen goals in each of the last six Premier League seasons! So, could he make it seven in a row? That was one of Mo's aims, but most importantly, he wanted to win more trophies with Liverpool.

In order to challenge Manchester City and Arsenal for the Premier League title again, the Reds had completely rebuilt their midfield over the summer of 2023. Big bids for Declan Rice and Moisés Caicedo had failed, but Alexis Mac Allister, Dominik Szoboszlai, Wataru Endō and Ryan Gravenberch had all arrived to add energy and creativity to the team.

The signs were good in pre-season, with lots of fast,

flowing football, and lots of goals. Now, could Liverpool play the same way in the Premier League?

Away at Chelsea, they started brilliantly. First, Mo hit the crossbar with a long-range strike, and then he dribbled in off the right wing and curled a beautiful pass through for Luis to slide in and score. *1–0!*

'Yesssssss!' Mo cheered, pumping his fists in the air. New season, same old superstar! And his key contributions continued in each and every game:

a rebound against Bournemouth,

the pass to set up Darwin's winning goal against Newcastle,

a flick finish against Aston Villa,

two killer crosses against Wolves,

a penalty against West Ham . . .

Whoa – Mo was on fire, with three goals and four assists in his first six games. What a start to the season!

His remarkable run finally came to an end away at Tottenham, which turned out to be a nightmare game for the whole Liverpool team. Two red cards, a last-minute own goal, and a 2–1 defeat – nooooooooo!

Never mind, the Reds came roaring back on the

attack in their next match against Brighton. The terrific team move started with Alexis on the halfway line,

who played the ball forward to Dominik,

who threaded it through to Luis,

who passed it left to Darwin,

who passed it right to Mo as he entered the box. From there, there was only going to be one result:

Goooooooooooooooooooooooooooooaaaaaaaaaaaaaaaaaaaaallllllllllllllllllllllllllllllllllllllllllll!!!!!!!!!!!!!!!!!

'Yessss, that's more like it!' Mo shouted with a serious, focused look on his face.

He added a second goal from the penalty spot before half-time, but unfortunately Liverpool couldn't hold onto their lead and the match finished in a frustrating 2–2 draw. Arghhh, two more precious points dropped! Oh well, at least Mo was in fantastic form ahead of the massive Merseyside derby . . .

Roared on by the loud crowd at Anfield, the Reds attacked again and again, but for the first seventy-five minutes, the Everton defence stood strong.

'Come on, Liverpool!' the supporters shouted, growing restless in the stands. They really needed a winning goal, but who was going to score it? Mo, of course! When Luis's cross struck Michael Keane on the arm, up stepped the Egyptian King to smash the penalty past Jordan Pickford. *1–0 at last!*

Everyone around him went wild, but Mo just calmly jogged away with his arms out wide. It was no big deal – after all, this was the seventh time he had scored in a Merseyside derby!

And he wasn't done yet. With seconds to go, Darwin burst forward on a last counter-attack and set up Mo to make it 2–0.

Goooooooooooooooooooooooooooaaaaaaaaaaaa aaaaaaaallllllllllllllllllllllllllllllllllllllll!!!!!!!!!!!!!!!!

Luis and Darwin both deserved lots of praise for their performances, but what would Liverpool do without their most lethal attacker of all?! It was Mo's seventh strike of the season already, and most importantly, the win put his team top of the table!

For now. By the end of the weekend, however, Tottenham, Arsenal and Manchester City had all climbed back above them again. Four teams, separated by just three points – the title race was well and truly on.

'Let's gooooooo!' Mo urged his teammates on ahead of their next game against Nottingham Forest. He had been in this high-pressure position many times before, and so he knew what Liverpool had to do: keep scoring and keep winning . . .

Midway through the first half, Mo slid a dangerous ball through to Darwin. His shot was saved, but Diogo was there to slam home the rebound. *1–0!*

Moments later, Mo played another defence-splitting pass, this time to Dominik, who cut the ball back for Darwin to score. *2–0!*

Liverpool's attackers were playing fantastic football together, and before the final whistle, Mo managed to add another goal of his own. Pouncing on a mix-up in the Forest defence, he coolly guided the ball into an empty net. *3–0!*

'Come onnnn!' Mo roared, throwing a fist in the air in front of the fans. With their Egyptian King in such fantastic form, it felt like Liverpool could achieve anything.

PHIL FODEN
STEPPING UP FOR CITY

What do you do next when you've already won everything? The answer for the Manchester City players was simple: go again and win more!

Yes, after achieving the Treble – the FA Cup, the Premier League and the UEFA Champions League – in 2022–23, Pep Guardiola's team were looking to do it all again in 2023–24. They wanted to win everything, but at the very top of their wishlist was lifting the Premier League title for a fourth year in a row. No club had ever done that, not even their big local rivals, Manchester United.

'Come on, we can do this!' Phil declared confidently when he returned for pre-season training.

Each season at City, Phil was getting better and better, and becoming more and more important to the team. Erling Haaland, Kevin De Bruyne and Rodri were still the superstars, but Phil was now not far behind.

Guardiola was a huge fan of his skill and work-rate, as well as his ability to shine in lots of different positions: midfield or attack; right, left, or centre.

'He can play anywhere,' the City manager liked to say.

For the 2023–24 season, however, Phil's aim was to push on and become one of the club's main superstars. At twenty-three, he wasn't a young player anymore. It was time for him to take his game to an even higher level. For the last three Premier League seasons, his stats had been consistently strong:

nine goals and five assists,

then nine goals and five assists again,

then eleven goals and five assists . . .

'But I know I can do better than that!' Phil told himself. He felt ready to step up for City, and the timing was perfect because his team were about to need him more than ever . . .

On the opening day of the new Premier League season, City travelled to Burnley and got off to the perfect start.

Phil to Bernardo Silva, to Kevin, to Rodri, to Erling . . . 1–0!

Easy! Twenty minutes later, however, the City smiles were suddenly turned upside down. After playing a pass, Kevin pulled up and put his hand in the air to signal to the bench that he was hurt and needed to come off.

Uh oh! Was it something serious? Yes – Kevin had injured his hamstring again and would need to have surgery. 'He'll be out for at least a few months,' Guardiola announced after the game.

A few months? Nooooooooo! What were City going to do without their main playmaker? Well, one thing was for sure: Phil needed to step up and fill the gap.

No problem!

He set up Julián Álvarez for the only goal against Newcastle,

and then Rodri to score a late winner against Sheffield United.

'Yessssssssss!' Phil cried out, throwing his arms up in the air.

It was so far, so good for City without Kevin. They were finding other ways to win every game:

Erling grabbed a hat-trick against Fulham,

New signing Jérémy Doku scored against West Ham, and against Nottingham Forest, Phil struck a fierce shot into the bottom corner for his first goal of the season.

'Come onnnnnn!' he yelled, pumping his fists in front of the Manchester City fans. Six wins out of six – were City just going to stroll their way to another Premier League title?

It was not going to be that simple. Away at Wolves, they suffered a shock 2–1 defeat, and then a week later, they also lost 1–0 to Arsenal.

'Nooooooooo!' At the final whistle, Phil sat down on the grass in disappointment – partly at the result, but also at his own performance. In City's biggest game of the season so far, he had failed to step up and fill the Kevin-shaped gap.

Zero shots,

Only thirty-three passes,

And only one big chance created.

'But I know that I can do better than that!' he thought to himself.

Oh well – there would be plenty more matches

for Phil to make a difference, starting with Brighton at home. Under Guardiola, City had never lost three league games in a row – was that record finally about to fall? No way!

City came flying out, straight from kick-off.

First, Jérémy raced up the left wing and crossed it for Julián. *1–0!*

Then Erling fired an unstoppable shot into the bottom corner. *2–0!*

'Get innnnnnn!' Phil shouted up into the sky. That was more like it from City! They were back to winning ways again – and just in time for the massive Manchester derby . . .

Although United were in poor form, their team was still packed with big-game superstars: Marcus Rashford, Rasmus Højlund, Christian Eriksen, Bruno Fernandes . . . Plus, they had home advantage at a sold-out Old Trafford, so City would have to stay calm and focused to get the derby won.

'Let's gooooooo!' Phil urged his teammates on while they waited in the tunnel. This time, he was determined to make a difference for City when they needed him most.

His first opportunity arrived inside the first ten minutes. When Kyle Walker played the ball across to him, Phil was unmarked on the edge of the six-yard box, but unfortunately, he couldn't quite get enough power on his header to beat the keeper.

'Oooooooohhhh!' Phil gasped with his hands on his head. What a great chance missed!

Never mind, City were soon ahead anyway, thanks to two goals from Erling. Late on, the striker had a great chance to complete his hat-trick, but instead, he unselfishly passed the ball across to . . . Phil! And this time, there was no way he could miss. *3–0!*

Goooooooooooooooooooooooooooaaaaaaaaaaaa aaaaaaaallllllllllllllllllllllllllllllllllllllll!!!!!!!!!!!!!!!!

'Yesssssssssss!' Phil screamed with delight, sliding towards the corner flag in celebration. The local kid from Stockport had just made sure that Manchester was blue once more.

That derby win left City in joint second place, two points off the top of the table. No problem at all, the Premier League season was a marathon, not a sprint.

Their experienced players knew exactly what they were doing, and there was plenty more to come – from Erling, from Kevin, and especially from Phil.

Pos	Team Name	Played	Wins	Draws	Losses	Goal Diff.	Points
1	**Tottenham Hotspur**	**10**	**8**	**2**	**0**	**13**	**26**
2	Arsenal	10	7	3	0	15	24
3	Manchester City	10	8	0	2	15	24

PART 2

PHIL FODEN A TALE OF TOO MANY DRAWS

When Manchester City thrashed Bournemouth 6–1 in early November and moved to the top of the Premier League table, some fans of other teams feared that was the title race already over.

'They'll just run away with it again now – BORING!'

It didn't turn out that way, though. With Kevin De Bruyne and John Stones both still out injured, City weren't the unstoppable force they used to be. Away at Chelsea, Rodri thought that he'd scored a late winner, but no – in the ninety-fifth minute, they conceded a penalty and up stepped their former player and Phil's good friend, Cole Palmer, to make it 4–4!

Owwww – that one really hurt, and so did the

disappointing results that followed:

Manchester City 1–1 Liverpool . . .

Again, they took the lead, and again, they gave away a late equaliser. Arghhhh, it felt like another game they should have won! It was frustrating, but Phil was determined to stay positive. 'Not the result we wanted but another point on the board,' he posted on social media, before moving onto the next match . . .

Manchester City 3–3 Tottenham . . .

When Phil made it 2–1 midway through the first half, it looked like City were in control of the match. But during the last twenty-five minutes of the game, they somehow let their lead slip . . . twice!

It was the same old story for City: a tale of too many draws. And before they improved, things were about to get even worse . . .

Aston Villa 1–0 Manchester City

Whoa, four Premier League games without a win. All of a sudden, City's season was falling apart! They were now six points behind the leaders, Arsenal, and down to fourth place because Villa had just overtaken them. If they didn't turn their form around soon, they could be out of the title race by Christmas!

Every single City player needed to raise their game, but Phil felt a particular responsibility. With only four goals and three assists in his first fifteen games, so far he had failed to fill the Kevin-shaped gap.

'But I know I can do better than that!' he told himself, turning frustration into motivation.

Phil couldn't solve City's problems straight away, though. After a nervy win over Luton, they let a two-goal lead slip against Crystal Palace. Oh dear, not again – another disappointing draw!

Perhaps a change of scene would help? In mid-December, the City players set off for Saudi Arabia to compete in the FIFA Club World Cup, and they returned a week later with their first trophy of the season. The first of many, Phil was hoping, as he got straight back to Premier League action. Before a short break in January, City still had two more matches to play, and he was determined to make it two more wins.

Away at Everton, they went 1–0 down, but which of their superstars sparked the fightback? Yes, Phil! With Erling out injured, he stepped forward with a crucial strike for City. Collecting the ball from Bernardo, he shifted it to the left and *BANG!* His fierce, low shot flew like an arrow into the bottom corner. *1–1!*

Gooooooooooooooooooooooooooooaaaaaaaaaaaaaaaaaaaaallllllllllllllllllllllllllllllllllllllllllllllllll!!!!!!!!!!!!!!!!

'That's more like it!' Phil thought to himself, but in the moment, he didn't show his delight. Instead, with a serious look on his face, he just turned and ran back for the restart, high-fiving his teammates along the way. Why the lack of celebration? Well, City still had work to do, and they got the job done, thanks to goals from Julián and Bernardo.

Phew! It was a real relief to get back to winning ways, and back into the Premier League top four. Now, could they end the year on a high with a victory against bottom club Sheffield United, at home at the Etihad?

From minute one, Phil was on fire, creating chance after chance for his team.

With a sublime touch, he flicked the ball back to Julián, but he dragged his shot wide. Nearly!

Never mind – a few minutes later, he laid the ball off to Rodri, who ran through and scored. *1–0!*

Before half-time, Phil weaved his way through the Sheffield United midfield with the ball glued to his left boot, and then played a defence-splitting pass through to Bernardo, but his strike was saved. Unlucky!

Never mind – in the second half, he burst into the box and set up Julián for a simple tap-in at the back post. *2–0!*

'Thanks, mate!' Julián called out, as he pointed and ran towards Phil, who was putting on his most magical performance of the season so far:

101 touches,

83 accurate passes out of 85,

6 chances created, and 2 assists.

Now those were numbers that even Kevin would be proud of!

'Phil has been outstanding,' his manager Guardiola praised him afterwards. 'Top, top, top class.'

Thanks, Boss! After a bad spell, things were suddenly looking much brighter for Manchester City. They were the new World Champions, they were still in the Premier League title race with a game in hand, and perhaps best of all, Phil was finding his best form at just the right time.

DECLAN RICE
DECLAN SAVES THE DAY (AGAIN)!

5 December 2023, Kenilworth Road, Luton

Watching Ross Barkley's shot roll under David Raya's diving body and into the net, Declan's shoulders slumped and his head dropped. How on earth had they let this happen? What on earth was going on? In the space of eight mad second-half minutes, Arsenal had gone from 2–1 up to 3–2 down!

Declan had done his best to stop the Luton attack by closing players down, but he couldn't do it all on his own! He needed more help from his teammates. Arsenal were usually so good at defending together as one big unit, with energy and organisation, but for once, they were too slow and sloppy. Did the players think that they were just going to beat Luton easily without putting in any effort? This was the Premier League!

Okay – enough negativity. After a moment of moaning and groaning to himself, Declan took a deep breath and got back to being his usual positive self. This was the wake-up call that Arsenal needed; now, they had to react. A quick look up at the clock on the stadium scoreboard told him that there were still more than thirty minutes to go.

'Come on, lads!' he clapped and cheered when the game kicked off again. 'There's still plenty of time to turn this around!'

Under Arteta, Arsenal had become a much stronger, more resilient team, who never gave up, no matter what. A disappointing defeat away at Newcastle in early November had ended their unbeaten start to the season, but the Gunners hadn't let that get them down. Instead, they had bounced straight back to winning ways against Burnley, Brentford and Wolves. Now, could they bounce back again to beat Luton and stay top of the table?

Just three minutes after conceding, Arsenal went up the other end and scored again. Bukayo lifted a high ball over the top to Gabriel Jesus, who used his strength to hold off the defender and then his skill to play a pass through to Kai. *3–3!*

'Get in, that's more like it, lads!' Declan shouted, jogging forward to join the team celebrations. Arsenal were level already, and they still had lots of time left to score another. Or so it seemed, but as the minutes ticked by, the winning goal just wouldn't come . . .

Martin's long-range strike was saved by the keeper,

Leandro Trossard blasted over from inside the box,

and the best chance of all fell to Kai, but his header was tipped over the bar.

Noooooooooooo!

The Gunners didn't give up, though, and they didn't panic either. 'We need to stay patient,' Martin told his teammates. 'If we keep calm, the goal will come!'

Yes, skipper! But as the match went into injury time, Declan did move further forward to join the attackers in the box. Arsenal didn't really need a deep defensive midfielder anymore, and Declan had already shown against Manchester United and Chelsea that he was capable of scoring big goals in big moments . . .

As Martin passed the ball left to Oleksandr

Zinchenko, Declan made a sudden dash towards the penalty spot, ready to attack any crosses that came in.

Now? No, Oleksandr passed it back to Martin, who curled it into the danger zone instead . . .

Now? Yes, Declan timed his leap to perfection, and then managed to direct his header down into the bottom corner. *4–3 to Arsenal!*

Gooooooooooooooooooooooooooaaaaaaaaaaaa aaaaaaaallllllllllllllllllllllllllllllllllllllll!!!!!!!!!!!!!!!!

Hurraaaaaaaay, he had done it – Declan the Arsenal hero had saved the day again! As the ball landed in the back of the net, he was off, racing over to jump and roar in front of the fans, followed by all of his delighted teammates.

'Last Minute Scenes!!' Declan posted on social media later that night, with a photo of him in that magical moment: arms out, mouth wide open, a massive smile spreading across his face. Amazing! It was a feeling, and a match, that Declan would never, ever forget. Thanks to him, the Gunners were still top and on track for the Premier League title!

Unfortunately, though, that Luton comeback wasn't

quite the inspiring turning point that Declan hoped it would be for Arsenal. Instead, the team continued to struggle, both in defence and up front. Losing 1–0 away at Aston Villa wasn't a total disaster, and neither was drawing 1–1 with Liverpool at Anfield, but losing at home against Declan's old club, West Ham? That really was a painful result!

Arsenal only had themselves to blame, though – they missed far too many chances in attack, and made too many mistakes at the back.

Emerson's cross into the box should have been dealt with easily, but instead Gabriel Magalhães and Oleksandr got in each other's way. The ball fell to Jarrod Bowen, who pulled it back for Tomáš Souček. *1–0!*

When the goal went in, Declan turned and walked away without saying a word. He didn't need to tell his teammates that they'd messed up; they already knew it. What the Gunners needed was a hero to step forward and save the day . . .

Early in the second half, Declan got the ball in the middle of the pitch, thirty yards from goal, and thought, 'Why not?' *BANG!* He fired off a ferocious shot that curled and dipped . . . but flew just over the crossbar. Ooooof, so close!

But just two minutes later, Konstantinos Mavropanos made it 2–0 to West Ham with a free header from a corner, and in the dying moments of the match, things nearly got even worse for Arsenal, especially for their defensive midfielder. Declan slipped as he intercepted a pass in his own box, and then as he tried to get the ball back, he sent Emerson flying. *Penalty!*

Declan didn't argue; he just looked down at the ground and shook his head. What a nightmare! The only good news was that David saved the spot-kick.

After that really disappointing performance, Arsenal dropped down to third place, behind Liverpool and Manchester City. Could they break their bad run away at Fulham, in their final match of 2023? No, this time, the Gunners didn't bounce straight back to winning ways. From 1–0 up, they fell to a 2–1 defeat. More missed chances, more defensive mistakes . . . oh dear, was this already the end of Arsenal's title hopes?

MO SALAH LEADING LIVERPOOL TO THE TOP

1 January 2024, Anfield, Liverpool

With a burst of speed, Dominik dribbled forward through the middle of the pitch, before poking a pass towards Darwin,

who dummied it for Luis . . .

. . . .who was expected to lay it across for Mo. But while unmarked on the right, Luis decided to go it alone, until he was eventually tripped by a Newcastle defender. *Penalty!*

'Now, I'll get my chance,' Mo thought to himself, while cheers rang out around Anfield. So far that season, he had taken all of Liverpool's spot-kicks in the Premier League, scoring three out of four. Was he now about to make it four out of five?

The home crowd certainly hoped so as Mo placed

the ball down on the spot. The Reds were on a brilliant run, unbeaten in their last twelve Premier League games. One more win here against Newcastle, and they would go top of the table – what a way to kick off the New Year!

After a short run-up, Mo blasted the ball with plenty of power . . . but straight at the goalkeeper. *SAVED!*

The rebound fell to Trent Alexander-Arnold . . . but he sliced his shot over the bar.

Noooooooo! Standing in the six-yard box, Mo ruffled his hair in frustration for a moment, but then he turned and got on with the game. Oh well, never mind, he'd missed – so what? No-one could succeed every time, not even him! There would be more chances to come in the match, and next time he would score, he was sure about that.

Despite the disappointment on New Year's Day, Mo had previously ended 2023 on continued fine form with two goals against Brentford, and then assists against Manchester City and Fulham. A week later, in early December against Crystal Palace, he had scored again, with a scruffy strike that was special for two reasons:

1) It was Mo's 200th goal for Liverpool, a total that only four other players had ever achieved at the club;

2) It led to a victory that lifted Liverpool to the top of the Premier League table!

Unfortunately, however, that triumph had only lasted one week. After draws against Manchester United and Arsenal, the Reds had then dropped back down to second place. But now Mo had another chance to lead his team back to the top, and despite missing that initial New Year penalty against Newcastle, he was determined to take it during the remainder of the game.

Early in the second half, Liverpool flew forward on the counter-attack again. Luis cut inside off the left wing and curled a perfect pass through to Darwin. He thought about shooting for goal himself, but instead decided to play the ball across to . . . Mo! This time, in the six-yard box, there was no way he was going to miss. *1–0!*

Gooooooooooooooooooooooooooaaaaaaaaaaaaaaaaaaaaallllllllllllllllllllllllllllllllllll!!!!!!!!!!!!!!!

After pointing a finger of thanks at Darwin, Mo decided to take a seat on top of the advertising boards behind the goal, his arms folded across his chest, as if he was just a supporter watching the game. Why? No-one really knew, but the new celebration did allow him to sit back and soak up that extra-special Anfield atmosphere.

Mo Salah! Mo Salah! Mo Salah! Running down the wing.
Mo Salah la-la-la la-ahh, the Egyptian king!

In that moment, he felt on top of the world and so glad that he'd stayed at Liverpool – but five minutes later, everything changed. Newcastle equalised, and suddenly Mo had more work to do.

No problem! From wide on the right, he dribbled infield towards the penalty area, teasing Dan Burn and tempting him to try and make a tackle. When he finally did, Mo slipped a sublime pass through the defender's legs to Diogo, who cut it back for Curtis Jones. *2–1!*

Hurraaaaay, Liverpool were leading again! Mo, however, was still hungry for more. Moments later, he chested the ball down and hit a beautiful cross with the outside of his left foot, which landed right at Cody's feet. *3–1!*

Game over? No, not yet. Newcastle scored again to give Liverpool a nervy last ten minutes. Could they stay strong and hold on for a crucial win? In fact, they did better than that. Alexis won the ball back deep in his own half and quickly launched a beautiful long pass to Diogo. He dribbled into the box and around the keeper, but as he did, his legs were clipped and he fell to the floor. *Another penalty to Liverpool!*

But the big question was: who would take it this time? The answer was . . . Mo again! Of course, he wanted another chance to score.

After taking a slightly longer run-up, he placed his shot low and hard into the bottom corner. It was an unstoppable spot-kick, even if the keeper had guessed the right way. *4–2!*

Goooooooooooooooooooooooooaaaaaaaaaaaaaaaaaaaallllllllllllllllllllllllllllllllllllllll!!!!!!!!!!!!!!!!

Now it really was game over! With two goals and an assist, Mo had successfully led Liverpool back to the top of the Premier League table!

What a superstar – what on earth would his team do without him? Unfortunately, they were about to find out because Mo had just played his last Premier League match for a while. He was heading off to the Ivory Coast to play for his country, Egypt, at the Africa Cup of Nations.

Pos	Team Name	Played	Wins	Draws	Losses	Goal Diff.	Points
1	**Liverpool**	**20**	**13**	**6**	**1**	**25**	**45**
2	Aston Villa	20	13	3	4	16	42
3	Manchester City	19	12	4	3	24	40

PART 3

DECLAN RICE ARSENAL'S NEW SET-PIECE SPECIALIST

After a really disappointing December, Arsenal had a two-week break in January and so manager Mikel Arteta decided to take his team to Dubai. They weren't there for a nice holiday, though, but to do some serious, warm-weather training, and to work out ways to improve for the second half of the season.

Arsenal's defending wasn't really the issue; it was their attacking, and most importantly of all, their scoring. Only four goals in their last five league games? Not good enough! Not when they had so many impressive young forwards, and not when they were trying to win the Premier League title. So, where else could they get some extra goals from?

'Set-pieces,' said Nicolas Jover, the club's set-piece coach. Arsenal had already used some clever corner-kick routines to score against Manchester United and Burnley, but Jover believed they could score a lot more. What they needed, however, was a new set-piece specialist. Gabriel Martinelli and Leandro Trossard were both good right-footed options, but maybe there was someone better, someone like . . . Declan?

During his last two seasons at West Ham, Declan had taken a lot of the team's set-pieces, and as Arteta and Jover discovered in Dubai, it was yet another area of football that he was very good at. In fact, when it came to delivering consistent, quality crosses into the box, Declan was Arsenal's best option.

'Okay, I think we should switch things up,' the coaches decided. Because of his height, they had mostly been using Declan as one of the big men in the middle, but not anymore. From now on, he would be the one taking the set-pieces.

So, would the new plan work? They would have to wait and see when Arsenal returned to Premier League action against Crystal Palace . . .

In the eleventh minute, Declan delivered his first high, curling corner towards the edge of the six-yard box, and up jumped Gabriel Magalhães to head the ball home. *1–0!*

'Come onnnnnn!' Declan cried out, rushing over to join in the team celebrations. The new plan was working already!

Arsenal went on to win the game 5–0 and they followed that up with victories over Nottingham Forest and Liverpool. Hurray, their title dream was alive again, and next up was the match that Declan had been waiting for: West Ham away. The defeat back in December still hurt, so it was time to return to his old home and put things right.

For the first thirty minutes, Arsenal attacked and attacked without scoring, but eventually the opening goal arrived from – yes, you guessed it – a corner! From the left, Declan delivered a perfect ball to the busy back-post area, where William Saliba hardly even had to jump. *1–0!*

After that, the Gunners absolutely hammered the Hammers. Bukayo scored the second, and Gabriel

Magalhães added a third from another deadly Declan set-piece, this time a free kick. That was two assists already, and midway through the second half, he scored a wondergoal to go with them. From outside the box, Declan blasted an unstoppable, first-time shot into the corner of the net. *6–0!*

Goooooooooooooooooooooooooooaaaaaaaaaaaaa aaaaaaaalllllllllllllllllllllllllllllllllll!!!!!!!!!!!!!!!!

Although he didn't outwardly celebrate out of respect for his old club, on the inside Declan was bursting with pride and joy. Tackles, interceptions, passes, goals, and now set-piece assists as well – he really was doing it all at the heart of the Arsenal midfield.

From there, the Gunners went on a real goal-scoring rampage:

5–0 away at Burnley,

4–1 at home against Newcastle,

6–0 away at Sheffield United . . .

Wow, that made it twenty-one goals in Arsenal's most recent four games! Meanwhile for Declan, it was four assists in his last four games, and six for the season, his best-ever total.

'I get excited by getting assists now,' he told the media after winning Premier League Player of the Year at the London Football Awards. 'It is a big thing for me.'

Being crowned Premier League Champions, however, was an even bigger thing, and Arsenal were now right back in the title race: one point behind Manchester City, and two behind Liverpool, but with the best goal difference of all.

'Come on, we can do this!' Declan told his teammates with confidence as they prepared to take on Brentford. It really felt like Arsenal were hitting their best form at just the right time.

With Jorginho sitting deeper in midfield, Arteta had given Declan the freedom to push further forward, and so that's what he did, making a late, bursting run into the box to head home from Ben White's cross. *1–0!*

Gooooooooooooooooooooooooooaaaaaaaaaaaa aaaaaaaalllllllllllllllllllllllllllllllllll!!!!!!!!!!!!!!!!

Declan raced over to the corner flag and then stood there, roaring up at the fans with the biggest grin on his face.

'Another one,' he wrote on social media afterwards.

Six goals and six assists – not bad at all for someone who was supposed to be a defensive midfielder! Declan was enjoying every second of his first season at Arsenal, but he was determined to end it on a high. A Premier League trophy high.

After beating Brentford in March, the Gunners moved to the top of the table, but their last match of the month was a massive one: Manchester City away. Lose and their title rivals would leave them trailing behind; win and they would have the advantage going into the last nine games. In the end, however, Arsenal did neither – instead, Declan and his teammates defended bravely and brilliantly to earn a 0–0 draw.

It wasn't a thrilling watch for Arsenal's fans, but what mattered more was winning the Premier League title, and with some help from their new set-piece specialist, Arsenal had now put themselves in an excellent position to do exactly that.

MO SALAH SERIOUS INJURIES AND SAD GOODBYES

At the Africa Cup of Nations, Mo carried on his excellent form for country as well as club. In Egypt's opening match against Mozambique, he stepped up to score a last-minute equaliser from the penalty spot. 2–2 – phew, what a calm-headed hero!

During Egypt's next match against Ghana, however, disaster struck. With half-time approaching, Mo suddenly waved to the referee and sat down on the grass holding his left leg. Uh oh, was it something serious? With a sad shake of the head, he had to hobble off the pitch.

Nooooooooo! And it wasn't just the worried Egypt fans who were crossing their fingers and toes; it was the Liverpool fans too. They really didn't want their top superstar striker to miss any more of the Premier League season!

The medical tests revealed that Mo had torn his hamstring, but he was determined to recover as quickly as possible. Would one week, or two weeks be enough? Hopefully! At first, he was aiming to return in time for the AFCON knock-out rounds, but sadly, his injury was taking too long to heal. So, with a heavy heart, Mo said goodbye and good luck to his national teammates, and flew back to England to carry on his recovery work.

Without their leader and top scorer, could Egypt still reach another AFCON final? Unfortunately not. They made it through the group stage, but in the Round of 16 they lost on penalties against the Democratic Republic of the Congo. Nooooooooo!

Meanwhile, what about Liverpool – were they missing Mo too? At the beginning, the answer appeared to be a big, loud 'NO!':

Bournemouth 0–4 Liverpool . . .

Two goals for Darwin, and two for Diogo.

. . . Liverpool 4–1 Chelsea . . .

Diogo, Dominik and Luis were all on the scoresheet, as well as the club's latest young star, Conor Bradley.

It was a stunning start to 2024, especially after the shock of some recent sad news. After nine amazing years, their beloved manager Jürgen Klopp had decided to leave at the end of the season!

At first, Mo couldn't believe what he was hearing; it was impossible to imagine life at Liverpool without him! But once the news had sunk in, those feelings soon switched to focus and determination. Together, the Liverpool players wanted to say goodbye by winning as many trophies as possible, including the Premier League title.

Next up, however, was a tough trip to Arsenal, and in the big game, Liverpool's only goal was an own goal as they lost 3-1. Okay, maybe they did miss Mo, after all!

The Reds managed to bounce back and beat Burnley without him, though, and by the time they faced Brentford in mid-February, Mo was fit enough to make the bench. Hurray! And when Diogo got injured just before half-time, on he came to make an instant impact . . .

First, from wide on the right, he slid a perfect pass across to Alexis in the middle. *2–0!*

'Yessssssssss!' the Argentinian yelled, throwing his arms around Mo.

Then, less than fifteen minutes after his assist, Mo scored a goal of his own. Racing on to Cody's flick-on, he showed the strength to hold off the defender and then the skill to curl a shot into the bottom corner. *3–0!*

Goooooooooooooooooooooooooooaaaaaaaaaaaaaaaaaaaallllllllllllllllllllllllllllllllllllllllll!!!!!!!!!!!!!!!!

'Welcome back!' Luis cheered happily, giving Mo a high-five and a hug.

It was a double-win day for Liverpool. Not only were they still top of the Premier League table, but their best attacking superstar was also back with a bang!

. . . Or was he? Despite that big, comeback performance against Brentford, Mo was still far from 100 percent fit, and so Klopp decided to rest him for the next two matches against Luton and Nottingham Forest. Luckily, Liverpool won both games without him, to hold on to the top spot ahead of facing formidable opponents: Manchester City at home at Anfield!

Oooof, the big one – there was no way Mo was going to miss it. Although he wasn't ready to start, he came racing on for the last thirty minutes. With the score tied at 1–1, could he make an instant impact for Liverpool again?

In his very first minute on the pitch, Mo collected the ball deep in his own half and split the City defence with a magical pass through to Luis. The Colombian was one-on-one with Ederson on the edge of the box . . . but under pressure and off balance, he blasted his shot just wide.

So close! Sadly, that turned out to be Liverpool's last golden chance to win the game. Oh well, a draw was still a good result against one of their title rivals, especially with ten games of the season still to play. Or ten games still to win, as Mo and his teammates preferred to think about it.

The first of those came at home against Brighton a few weeks later, where Mo was finally ready to return to the Liverpool starting line-up again. Hurray! And even though they went 1–0 down after ninety seconds, the players and supporters never stopped believing, because every time Mo touched the ball, he looked so dangerous. He curled his first shot wide, then volleyed the next one over the bar. *Nearly!* It was surely only a matter of time before he got Liverpool back into the game . . .

In fact, it was Luis who poked in the equaliser, but it all came from Mo's clever header back into the box, and midway through the second half, the Egyptian King finally scored a second of his own. As the pass from Alexis arrived at his feet, Mo found himself unmarked inside the Brighton box. Danger alert! A golden chance to be the match-winner? There was no way he was going to miss that. *2–1!*

Gooooooooooooooooooooooooooaaaaaaaaaaaa aaaaaaaallllllllllllllllllllllllllllllllllllllllll!!!!!!!!!!!!!!!!

For a moment, Mo just stood there in front of the fans with his arms out wide, soaking up the special Anfield atmosphere. What a hero – right when his team needed him most in the Premier League title race, he was back once again with a bang!

. . . Or was he?

PHIL FODEN
CITY'S HAT-TRICK HERO

At the start of the new year, there was exciting news for all Manchester City fans: Kevin De Bruyne was finally fit and ready to make his big comeback, just in time for the most important part of the season! He was such a key player for the team, and on his Premier League return, he came off the bench to help them beat Newcastle with a goal and an assist.

'Buzzin' with the win,' Phil posted afterwards. 'Nice to have you back @kevindebruyne'.

But with the Belgian back in the squad, what did that mean for Phil's own future? In the past when the two of them had played together, Kevin had been the main man, with Phil as his promising young assistant, but surely those roles were about to change? Because they were both real City superstars now!

Sure enough, in their next league match against Burnley, they shone brightly together in the same starting line-up. Kevin set up City's second goal with a killer pass to Julián, and then Phil set up the third with a weaving run and pass to Rodri.

'Mate, you're on fire!' the Belgian cheered as they celebrated with a hug. What a deadly double act they were! Instead of shying away since Kevin's return, Phil was playing with even more confidence and taking his game to the next level, that of world-class.

A week later against Brentford, City went 1–0 down, but they soon came fighting back, and who led the way? Phil, with a little help from his older assistant! Kevin's cross into the box was cleared away, but only as far as Phil, who calmly chested the ball down and slotted it past the keeper. *1–1!*

Goooooooooooooooooooaaaaaaaaalllllllllllllllllllllll!

As he turned to run back for the restart, Phil decided to show off a new celebration. Crouching down on one knee, he stretched both arms out in front of him and pretended to fire a gun with them. Why? Well, his teammates had started calling him 'The Sniper' because of his brilliant shooting in training, and now he was doing it in matches too!

Early in the second half, City's deadly double act teamed up again. Kevin curled the ball in from the left, and Phil made a smart run from right to centre, to score with a low flick header. *2–1!*

'Get innnnnnnnn!' This time, he celebrated with a knee slide over to the corner flag first, followed by 'The Sniper' once he was back on his feet. What next? Phil was on a hat-trick now!

When Rodri's pass rolled towards him, he decided to dummy it and let it run through to Erling. Then, when his teammate tapped it across first time, *ZOOM!* Phil burst forward into the gap that had just opened up in the Brentford defence, with the ball glued to his left boot. It was fast, flowing football at its best, and Phil finished the move off in style by steering a shot past the keeper. *3–1!*

Hurray, he was a hat-trick hero! With his arms out wide, Phil stood in front of the fans, nodding his head as if to say, 'Yeah, I'm a real City superstar now!'

He wasn't the only one, though, and that's what made them so unstoppable. Erling scored both goals to beat Everton, and the winner in the return match against Brentford too. Then against Bournemouth, it was Phil to the rescue once again, tapping in the rebound after Erling's shot had been saved.

As for the big Manchester derby against United in early March? The win was a real team effort, but there was no doubt who their man of the match was: Phil!

As the second half ticked by, City found themselves 1–0 down and in desperate need of a moment of magic. No problem! When Phil got the ball on the right, he dribbled inside to make more space and then *BANG!* He fired off a stunning shot that rose higher and higher, into the top corner. *1–1!*

Goooooooooooooooooooaaaaaaaaallllllllllllllllllllll!

What a strike! As he celebrated in front of the fans, however, Phil didn't show that much emotion, because he was a man on a mission, with more work still to do. To win the Premier League title for a record fourth time in a row, City needed all three points, so he carried on attacking until eventually another scoring chance arrived. After playing a one-two with Julián, Phil burst into the box and then coolly guided the ball around the keeper and into the far bottom corner. *2–1!*

He was the Manchester derby match-winner! Phil went wild, waving his arms around and screaming at the top of his voice while he raced over to the corner flag. For a local kid from Stockport, it was the ultimate dream come true.

That night, he summed the feeling up perfectly in his social media post: 'Derby day delight!' His manager, meanwhile, summed up the thoughts of the football world perfectly: 'He is the best player in the Premier League right now.'

It was an incredible thing to hear, but Phil wasn't getting carried away. City were still one point behind Liverpool at the top of the table, and they were about to face them away at Anfield. Matches didn't get any more difficult; so could Phil create another moment of magic to score another big goal in another big game?

John Stones gave City the lead from a clever corner-kick routine, before Liverpool equalised from the penalty spot early in the second half. With forty minutes to go, it was 1–1 – the scene was perfectly set for a hero to step forward . . .

While Kevin controlled the ball on the edge of the

Liverpool box, Phil pulled into space on the right and called for the pass. When it arrived, he dribbled away from the defender and into the area . . . but instead of coolly slotting his shot into the far corner like he had against Manchester United, or crossing it to Erling in the middle, Phil fired it straight at the keeper. *Saved!*

Noooooooo – what a great chance wasted! In the end, the match finished in a draw, and there was even more frustration to come in City's next match, a tough battle at home against Arsenal. Other than one blocked shot, Phil hardly made an impact at all, and after sixty minutes, his manager decided to sub him off.

Dull as the 0–0 draw was to watch, at least City had one more point to add to their total and they had now gone fourteen league games without defeat. That was a very worrying stat for their two title rivals . . .

Pos	Team Name	Played	Wins	Draws	Losses	Goal Diff.	Points
1	**Liverpool**	**29**	**20**	**7**	**2**	**40**	**67**
2	Arsenal	29	20	5	4	46	65
3	Manchester City	29	19	7	3	35	64

PART 4

MO SALAH NO PERFECT PREMIER LEAGUE ENDING

With nine games left of the season, Liverpool had a two-point lead at the top of the Premier League table. Could they hold on to lift the title for the second time in five years? What a perfect ending to the Klopp era that would be!

The signs looked promising as the Reds picked up all three points against Sheffield United. Darwin was scoring goals, Alexis was running the show, and one by one, their most important injured stars were returning: first Mo, then Andy Robertson and Curtis Jones – and soon Trent would be ready to make his comeback too. Hurray, just in time to lead Liverpool to the title!

That was the plan, but unfortunately, their old rivals

Manchester United had other ideas. Away at Old Trafford, Liverpool were on fire in the first half, creating chance after chance. At half-time, however, they only had one goal to show for all their fantastic football because their attackers had failed to take their chances.

Dominik's first shot was saved by André Onana, and his second flew wide,

then Darwin missed from a dangerous position,

and so, unusually, did Mo. Twice!

Whoa, what was going on? Would Liverpool regret all those wasted opportunities? Yes – early in the second half, Jarell Quansah made one mistake and suddenly Manchester United were level. Then, fifteen minutes later, they scored again to take the lead. *2–1!*

Liverpool were heading for a disastrous defeat, unless a hero could save the day . . .

With only five minutes left, Mo played a first-time pass through to Harvey Elliott as he entered the box, and the United defender got his tackle all wrong. *Penalty!*

There was no question about who would take it for Liverpool. Pressure, what pressure?! After a big, deep breath, Mo shuffled a few steps to the right and then ran forward . . . and sent the keeper the wrong way.

Goooooooooooooooooooooooooooooaaaaaaaaaaaaaaaaaaaallllllllllllllllllllllllllllllllll!!!!!!!!!!!!!!!!

It was 2–2 – phew! At least they hadn't lost the game, but still, the Liverpool players left the pitch feeling very disappointed. They'd taken twenty-eight shots, but the result was only two goals, and only one point.

'The draw feels like a defeat,' Virgil admitted afterwards, and Mo totally agreed with his captain. Oh well, onto the next one . . .

It was clear that Liverpool needed to be a lot more clinical, but at home against Crystal Palace, it was the same story all over again. Only this time, the ending was even worse: 21 shots, no goals, and no points.

'Nooooooooooo!' Mo moaned, throwing his arms up in frustration as his late shot was blocked by a Palace defender. At the most important stage of the Premier League season, Liverpool were losing their nerve and losing games. They were down to third place now, and with Arsenal and Manchester City both in unbeatable form, one more defeat could spell the end of their title challenge altogether . . .

With the pressure on, Liverpool bounced back to win 3–1 at Fulham, but next up was a massive Merseyside derby, away at Goodison Park. No-one would enjoy ending their trophy dream more than their local rivals Everton – and unfortunately that's exactly what happened.

For all their twenty-three shots, Liverpool's attackers failed to score from a single one. Luis hit the bar, Darwin fired straight at the keeper, and Mo, unusually, missed the target. Three times. Whoa, what was going on?!

At the other end of the pitch, meanwhile, Liverpool's defending was all over the place, and Everton took full advantage. In the first half, Jarrad Branthwaite tapped in after an ugly goal-mouth scramble, and then in the second, Dominic Calvert-Lewin jumped highest to double their lead.

'NOOOOOOOOOOO!' Mo yelled, thrashing at the air in anger. After all their hard work all season, they had thrown it away!

Oh dear, it was game over, and season over for Liverpool. With four Premier League matches to go, the three-team title race was now down to two . . .

DECLAN RICE FIGHTING UNTIL THE FINAL DAY

In mid-April, Arsenal also looked like a team in title trouble. On the same day as Liverpool's shock defeat to Crystal Palace, the Gunners suffered a setback of their own. After comfortable wins against Luton and Brighton, they came unstuck at home against Aston Villa.

With fifteen minutes to go, the game was heading for a 0–0 draw, but instead of settling for one point, Declan and his teammates pushed forward in search of all three. That turned out to be a big mistake, because Villa scored two late goals to win the game instead.

What a crushing blow! Was this the end of Arsenal's Premier League title challenge? No way! According to Declan, it was just another wake-up call.

'If you can't win games of football, don't lose,' he said, with frustration in his voice and on his face. 'But look, we've got six finals to go, and we'll give it everything.'

Having learned their lesson against Villa, the Gunners kept fighting – and winning – all the way until the final day of the season:

Wolves 0–2 Arsenal,

Arsenal 5–0 Chelsea . . .

What a win, and it all started with yet another Declan assist. Now that defensive midfielder Thomas Partey was back from injury at last, he had even more freedom to attack, and so in only the fourth minute, he dribbled forward on a powerful run into the Chelsea box, before slipping it left for Leandro to shoot and score. *1–0!*

'Yessssss!' Declan cheered, clenching his fists in front of the fans. With his help, his team were on their way to another huge victory.

Tottenham 2–3 Arsenal . . .

Nothing was going to stop the Gunners now, not even a massive North London derby, away at the Tottenham Hotspur Stadium. By half-time, Arsenal were already 3–0 up, with their new set-piece specialist setting up the third goal for Kai with another amazing corner-kick.

'Come onnnnnnn!' Declan cried out with passion,

when the ball landed in the net. It was his eighth league assist of the season. Surely victory was now theirs?

Although Tottenham fought back brilliantly in the second half, Arsenal stayed strong and held on for all three precious points. Phew! Only three must-win matches left now – their title hopes remained alive…

Arsenal 3–0 Bournemouth . . .

After slicing a shot wide in the first half, Declan recovered in the second half, like a true superstar. First, he set up Leandro with a calm, clever flick, and then in the very last minute, he scored one of his own.

When Gabriel Martinelli launched Arsenal's counter-attack, Declan was back defending deep in his own half, but with one final burst of energy, *ZOOM!* He sprinted forward, from one box to the other.

'Yesss!' he called out to Gabriel Jesus, pointing ahead to where he wanted the pass. When it arrived, Declan's first touch took him a bit wide, but no problem – he still managed to fire the ball past the keeper and into the net from a really tight angle. *3–0!*

Goooooooooooooaaaaaaaaallllllllllllllllllllllllll!!!!!!!

What an all-round midfield masterclass! With a huge

smile on his face, Declan jogged over to the corner flag and then stopped to salute the Arsenal supporters. Job done! Premier League title dream still alive!

With their rivals Manchester City winning game after game, all they could was keep doing the same . . .

Manchester United 0–1 Arsenal . . .

Away at Old Trafford, the Gunners weren't at their best, but they still got the match won, and that was all that really mattered. Once Leandro's early goal went in, their victory never looked in doubt. Declan and Thomas bossed the midfield area together, and behind them, the defence was as solid as ever.

When the final whistle blew, Arsenal moved back to the top of the Premier League table. But there were no real celebrations from Declan and his teammates, because Manchester City were only one point behind and they still had a game in hand.

Even so, no matter how the season ended, the Arsenal players could feel so proud of their fighting spirit. Since losing to Villa in April, they had bounced back to win every single match, taking the Premier League title race all the way to the final day.

PHIL FODEN
MORE WINS, MORE MAGIC

How does a real superstar respond after getting subbed off early? By scoring a hat-trick in his next game! Just four days after that disappointing 0–0 draw against Arsenal, Phil was back in the Manchester City starting line-up to face Aston Villa. Kevin and Erling were both on the bench, so it was a big test of whether the team could still win without them.

As half-time approached, the match was tied at 1–1, when City won a free kick in a brilliant shooting position. So which of their many superstars would take it? Jack and Julián were standing around the ball too, but there was really only one man for the job. After a deep breath, Phil ran up and curled a shot through the Villa wall and into the back of the net. *2–1!*

Gooooooooooooooooooooooooooooaaaaaaaaaaaa aaaaaaaaallllllllllllllllllllllllllllllllllll!!!!!!!!!!!!!!!

Whoa, what a beauty and it was Phil's twelfth of the

season, his best-ever total in the Premier League!

And there was plenty more magic to come. In the second half, Phil burst into the box to collect a pass from Rodri and swept the ball first time into the bottom corner. *3–1!*

It was an inch-perfect finish, in off the post, and just five minutes later, he was celebrating his second hat-trick of the season. Phil was sure that he'd been fouled on the edge of the Villa box, but when the referee said no, he quickly picked himself up, rushed in to win the ball back, and then fired an unstoppable strike into the top corner. *4–1!*

Gooooooooooooooooooooooooooaaaaaaaaaaaaaaaaaaaallllllllllllllllllllllllllllllllllllllllllll!!!!!!!!!!!!!!!

HAT-TRICK! With his tongue out and his finger wagging in the air, Phil raced away to celebrate with the wildly cheering fans. He was having the time of his life as City's number one superstar!

The next day's headlines read 'FANTASTIC FODEN'. At the most important stage of the season, he was just getting better and better.

But with City also chasing Champions League glory,

Guardiola decided to rest Phil for three of their next four Premier League matches. Although the team still managed to keep winning without him, they always played better when he was out there on the pitch.

Away at Brighton, Phil came back with a double *BANG! BANG!* his free kick flew off a defender and into the net, and then *BANG!* he calmly guided the ball into the bottom corner after some excellent City pressing.

Phil just couldn't stop scoring! He had now passed fifteen goals for the season, and fifty Premier League goals in total. He was on a remarkable run, and so were his team. City were now unbeaten in eighteen games, with four wins in a row, and even more to come:

Nottingham Forest 0–2 Manchester City,

Manchester City 5–1 Wolves . . .

Erling was the man of this match, but Phil also played his part, setting up the striker's fourth goal with a beautifully chipped pass from deep inside his own half.

Fulham 0–4 Manchester City . . .

With his team winning 1–0, Phil made sure of the victory by sweeping the ball into the bottom corner, this time with his weaker right foot.

Goooooooooooooooooooooooooooooaaaaaaaaaaaa aaaaaaaalllllllllllllllllllllllllllllllllllllll!!!!!!!!!!!!!!!!!

'Come onnnnnnnn!' Phil roared in celebration in front of the City fans. Yet again, he had produced a moment of magic, just when his team needed it most.

The victory took City back to the top of the Premier League table, but their lead only lasted for 24 hours. Why? Because while they were winning game after game, so were their title rivals Arsenal.

1	*Arsenal*	*37*	*86pts*
2	*Manchester City*	*36*	*85pts*

The main difference, however, was that City still had an extra match left to play before the final day . . .

Tottenham 0–2 Manchester City . . .

The first big chance of the night fell to Phil, but as the ball dropped down to him on the edge of the six-yard box, he couldn't quite lift his volley over the long arms of the Tottenham keeper. *SAVED!*

What a missed opportunity! Never mind, City were so strong that if one of their superstars failed, another one was sure to succeed. Early in the second half, Bernardo slipped a pass through to Kevin, who crossed it in for Erling . . . *1–0!*

'Yesssssss!' Phil yelled, throwing his arms up in the air. City had the crucial first goal they needed, and in the final minutes, he helped make a second. From Erling's flick-on, Phil blasted a long ball forward, but he didn't just hit and hope; he cleverly played it over the top of the Tottenham defence for Jérémy to chase. The speedy winger won the race with ease, and as he dribbled into the box, he was fouled. *Penalty!*

Up stepped Erling and . . . *2–0!*

The striker walked coolly over towards the fans, and Phil was already there in front of them, jumping and down with delight. Because City were so nearly there now, so close to a record-breaking fourth Premier League title in a row. Just one more game to go; just one more win . . .

Before that, however, Phil had some very important individual awards to collect. For his seventeen goals, eight assists, and countless moments of magic, he had been named the Football Writers' Association Footballer of the Year AND the Premier League Player of the Season.

'What a week!' he posted on social media alongside some happy, smiling photos. 'So honoured to receive these prestigious awards! Thank you to everyone who voted for me, to the City staff and coaches, my family, and of course, my teammates.'

Phil's superstar season wasn't over yet, though. There were still more moments of magic ahead.

Pos	Team Name	Played	Wins	Draws	Losses	Goal Diff.	Points
1	**Manchester City**	**37**	**27**	**7**	**3**	**60**	**88**
2	Arsenal	37	27	5	5	61	86
3	Liverpool	37	23	10	4	43	79

THE FINAL DAY

19 May 2024, 4:00pm

Manchester City vs West Ham, Etihad Stadium
Arsenal vs Everton, Emirates Stadium

2 MINUTES, ETIHAD STADIUM

A strong start was what City wanted, and a strong start was exactly what they got. Out on the right wing, Bernardo looked up for a pass to play, and heard someone calling for the ball in the middle: Phil! When it rolled towards him, a West Ham defender rushed in to make a tackle, but he was ready for that. With a swivel of his body and a beautiful first touch, Phil shifted the ball across into space on the edge of the box and . . . *BANG!* His shot flew into the top corner in a flash. *1–0!*

Gooooooooooooooooooooooooooooooaaaaaaaaaaaa aaaaaaaallllllllllllllllllllllllllllllllllllllllll!!!!!!!!!!!!!!!!

What a screamer, and what a day to score it! Phil was so pumped up that he went for three celebrations in one: first the arms out wide, then the knee slide, and finally, the corner flag smash.

'Come onnnnnnnnn!'

5 MINUTES, EMIRATES STADIUM

An early goal was what Arsenal really needed, especially after the bad news coming from the Etihad Stadium. With his pathway blocked by three Everton defenders, Martin looked up and laid the ball back to Declan, who curled in a brilliant first-time cross from the edge of the box. It was too high for Thomas and for Gabriel Magalhães too, but it was perfect for Takehiro Tomiyasu, who had snuck in at the back post . . .

BOOM! He headed it down, but the ball flew just wide of the far post. So close! Oh well, at least Arsenal still had lots of time left . . .

18 MINUTES, ETIHAD STADIUM

Manchester City, meanwhile, were a team on a title-winning mission, and they wanted to complete it as quickly as possible. After Erling dropped deep and laid the ball off to Jérémy, *ZOOM!* Phil was off, bursting into the West Ham box like a striker. And when the cross came in, he finished like a striker too, calmly curling a first-time shot into the bottom corner. *2–0!*

Gooooooooooooooooooooooooooooaaaaaaaaaaaa aaaaaaaallllllllllllllllllllllllllllllllllllllllll!!!!!!!!!!!!!!!!

Phil was on fire on the final day, just like he had been all season! This time, he celebrated like a confident superstar, pointing to his chest and then down at the pitch as if to say, 'This is where I belong, and look what I can do!'

40 MINUTES, EMIRATES STADIUM

As half-time approached, Arsenal were a team in trouble. Dominic Calvert-Lewin had already hit the post, and now Everton had a free kick in a dangerous position. At first, Idrissa Gueye's strike looked like it was going high and wide, but then it flicked off a player in the wall and flew into the far side of the net. *1–0!*

Noooooo – and which unlucky Arsenal star had deflected the shot with his head? Declan! As he turned and watched the ball hit the net, his heart sank. Was that it, the end of their title dream?

42 MINUTES, ETIHAD STADIUM

Oooooh, wait a second, Arsenal supporters – maybe City hadn't secured the Premier League title just yet! Their defenders failed to clear a West Ham corner-kick, and Mohammed Kudus scored with an incredible overhead kick. 2–1 – game on!

59 MINUTES, ETIHAD STADIUM

City were still on track to be crowned Premier League Champions again, but another goal would certainly make things more comfortable. At the end of another slick passing move, Kevin played the ball through to Bernardo, who laid it back to Rodri, who guided a shot past the keeper from the edge of the penalty area. *3–1!*

Phew! This time, it really was game over at the Etihad Stadium, and the title race was over too.

95 MINUTES, ETIHAD STADIUM

It was all over, and Manchester City had done it; they had won the Premier League title again, for a record-breaking fourth season in a row! As their fans stormed the pitch, Phil and his teammates rushed back to the changing room to get the party started.

Campeones, Campeones, Olé! Olé! Olé!

What a feeling, and what a moment!

'HISTORY MAKERS,' Phil posted a week later, once

the trophy had been kissed, lifted, and then taken through the streets of Manchester on an open-top bus parade. 'An incredible season comes to an end.'

PREMIER LEAGUE FINAL TABLE							
Pos	Team Name	Played	Wins	Draws	Losses	Goal Diff.	Points
1	**Manchester City**	**38**	**28**	**7**	**3**	**62**	**91**
2	Arsenal	38	28	5	5	62	89
3	Liverpool	38	24	10	4	45	82
4	Aston Villa	38	20	8	10	15	68
5	Tottenham Hotspur	38	20	6	12	13	66
6	Chelsea	38	18	9	11	14	63
7	Newcastle United	38	18	6	14	23	60
8	Manchester United	38	18	6	14	-1	60
9	West Ham United	38	14	10	14	-14	52
10	Crystal Palace	38	13	10	15	-1	49
11	Brighton & Hove Albion	38	12	12	14	-7	48
12	Bournemouth	38	13	9	16	-13	48
13	Fulham	38	13	8	17	-6	47
14	Wolverhampton Wanderers	38	13	7	18	-15	46
15	Everton	38	13	9	16	-11	40
16	Brentford	38	10	9	19	-9	39
17	Nottingham Forest	38	9	9	20	-18	32
18	*Luton Town*	*38*	*6*	*8*	*24*	*-33*	*26*
19	*Burnley*	*38*	*5*	*9*	*24*	*-37*	*24*
20	*Sheffield United*	*38*	*3*	*7*	*28*	*-69*	*16*

PREMIER LEAGUE TOP SCORERS				
		Goals	Assists	Games
1	Erling Haaland	27	5	31
2	Cole Palmer	22	11	34
3	Alexander Isak	21	2	30
4=	Ollie Watkins	19	13	37
4=	Phil Foden	19	8	35
4=	Dominic Solanke	19	3	38
7	Mohammed Salah	18	10	32
8	Son Heung-Min	17	10	35
9=	Bukayo Saka	16	9	35
9=	Jarrod Bowen	16	6	34
9=	Jean-Philippe Mateta	16	5	35

TOP 5 YOUNG PLAYERS

Few things in football are more exciting than a young player coming from nowhere to take the team by storm. Powered by the spirit of youth, these are the fearless risk-takers who have shone in the limelight this season. While Jude Bellingham and Cole Palmer undoubtedly stood amongst the very best, the following five players also transformed their teams and outwitted their opponents.

1 FLORIAN WIRTZ (BAYER LEVERKUSEN)

The Bundesliga player of the season pulled the strings for the undefeated German champions. With 18 goals and 19 assists, the German wonderkid often made all the difference to one of Leverkusen's all-time great seasons. In his first full season back fit after a devastating ACL injury, Wirtz proved himself comfortable anywhere in attack. Always happy to receive the ball under pressure, he was exceptional at finding defence-splitting passes.

But it wasn't just Wirtz's on-ball creativity that tore teams apart. His intelligent movement created plenty of space for his teammates, while his work rate in defence saw him run further than almost all other players in the league, allowing his teammates to press aggressively to win the ball back.

2 SALMA PARALLUELO (FC BARCELONA FEMENÍ)

Aged twenty, Paralluelo placed third in the Ballon d'Or, and with another season under her belt, her sights may now be set even higher. The Barcelona winger has caused havoc once more with 32 goals and nine assists in 2023–24. Formerly a champion hurdler at youth level in Spain, she overcame all obstacles with her pace, intelligence and finishing. Twice, she scored four goals in one game (against Sevilla and Real Sociedad), and her six Champions League goals proved vital as Barcelona retained their title once more.

3 LAMINE YAMAL (BARCELONA)

At just sixteen years of age, Yamal didn't just arrive on the world stage. He dominated. Clearly establishing himself in Barcelona's starting eleven, the talented teenager made fifty appearances, scored seven goals and made seven assists.

His left-footed strike against Real Mallorca earned him La Liga's goal of the month, and was typical of his style. Happiest when cutting in from the right wing to shoot on his left foot, Yamal also proved himself capable of finding teammates with crosses. An exceptional ball striker, impressive dribbler and confident passer, there are few defenders who can deal with this teenage talent.

4 ENDRICK (PALMEIRAS)

Having spent time in an orphanage after his parents were unable to feed him, the young Endrick was determined to become a professional footballer to help his family. In 2023–24, the forward not only achieved his goal; he smashed it! After becoming the youngest player to ever play for Palmeiras in the 2022–23 season, he went on to win the league title with them, scoring eleven goals (more than any other U18 player in Serie A history – except for Ronaldo Nazário).

Already known globally as a promising talent, Endrick truly announced himself on the world stage by scoring the winner for Brazil in a friendly against England.

Confident and powerful with a deadly left foot and a box of tricks that can bamboozle any defender, Endrick is an excellent finisher but also happy linking play. His talent proved so great that Spanish giants Real Madrid were convinced to pay a fee of up to £60 million (that should certainly be able to help out his family!). With

Endrick due to line up in the white of Los Blancos next season, the whole world will be watching in anticipation.

4 KHIARA KEATING (MANCHESTER CITY WOMEN)

It's hard enough to break through as a young talent, but to do so as a goalkeeper? Well, that's really tough. In a position where experience and physicality has traditionally been valued highly, Khiara Keating proved herself more than capable. After playing just three games for Manchester City in the 2022–23 season, she made the number one spot her own with some fine displays – particularly against Arsenal in a 1–0 victory in the FA Cup. Keeping nine clean sheets in twenty-two league games, Keating became the youngest player to ever win the WSL Golden Glove. The outstanding shot-stopper's performances were rewarded with a first England call-up. It surely won't be her last . . .

WOMEN'S SUPER LEAGUE

INTRODUCTION

This is the story of an epic battle between two top sides, Chelsea Women and Manchester City Women over a gruelling season. The 2023–24 season in the Women's Super League will go down as one of the most nail-biting contests in the league's history, with almost too many twists and turns along the way to tell you about!

Both teams were relying on their star players to deliver when it mattered. Would Chelsea's explosive young forward, Lauren James, a brilliant baller who still had lots to learn, be crowned a champion, or could City's super striker Khadija 'Bunny' Shaw claim her first trophy?

So who *did* win the title and just how was it won? Sky blue or royal blue? Bunny or Lauren? If you're ready to join these Ultimate Football Heroes on their journeys, read on!

CHAPTER 1

BACK IN BUSINESS

1 Oct 2023, Stamford Bridge, London

As Lauren James stood by the centre circle at Chelsea's Stamford Bridge stadium, a wave of excitement rippled through her body. A brand-new season in the Women's Super League was about to kick off, and she couldn't wait to get started.

Chelsea had been champions four times in a row now, and since manager Emma Hayes had brought her to the club, Lauren had won a hat-trick of medals. Still only just twenty-two, she had become one of Chelsea's most important players. Nevertheless, a huge season lay ahead, one in which Lauren had to show more than just flashes of her genius. It was time to kick on and perform week in, week out, over eight exhausting months.

Less than six weeks earlier, Lauren had played in the biggest match of her life, when England had narrowly lost the Women's World Cup final to Spain. Some fans and pundits had said Lauren hadn't deserved to play at all, after her disastrous red card and a two-match ban for the Lionesses earlier in the competition. A moment of madness had seen Lauren's emotions get the better of her and she had been rightly sent off for kicking out at an opponent.

I can't let that happen again, Lauren told herself. She wanted to be a player that her teammates could rely on.

Back at Chelsea, Emma had helped patch up her star player, reminding Lauren of all the positives from the tournament in Australia. 'You had the world at your feet!' Emma had told her young forward. Lauren's three goals and three assists for England were proof of that. 'You're not the first footballer to make a mistake,' Emma went on, 'and you certainly won't be the last.'

Lauren felt lucky to always have her manager on her

side, and the Chelsea fans never stopped singing her name. She hoped she could make them proud. Every time she played at Stamford Bridge, the club's main stadium, she usually made something special happen. And with her brother Reece – also a Chelsea star – in the crowd, she hoped she had more magic in her boots that day.

Chelsea looked dangerous from the start against London rivals Tottenham Hotspur. Lauren forced Spurs keeper Becky Spencer into a diving save early on, before shooting over the bar soon after. Close!

It was the Blues' new signing Mia Fishel who opened the scoring, though, rising highest to head home Niamh Charles's corner.

After the break, Lauren came closer still – this time only the crossbar saved Spurs' blushes.

Some players would start to think it wasn't their day. Not Lauren, though. She kept making her runs and carving out chances, determined to add to the score.

Chelsea continued to pile on the pressure, with Guro Reiten certain her tap-in had crossed the line before Spurs scrambled the shot away.

Guro saw the funny side. 'Where's VAR when you need it?'

With the ball still in play, Niamh clipped a pass back in to Lauren, who connected perfectly with her right boot. *Gooooaaaalllll!* A beautiful volley showed exactly what Lauren was all about. She sprinted to the corner flag to celebrate with the fans, before her teammates squashed her in an enormous blue huddle.

'Yes, LJ!' cheered Chelsea captain Millie Bright. 'What a finish!'

Lauren's face lit up. She waved to Reece in the stands.

Spurs struck back late on, but Chelsea never looked in danger. Three points in the bag on their journey to try to win an unmatched fifth league title in a row. Was it an impossible task? Time would tell.

Further north, Manchester City definitely wanted a say in where the trophy would end up. The Sky Blues had only added one summer signing, Dutch midfielder Jill Roord, although their squad already oozed quality. Lionesses Lauren Hemp, Alex Greenwood and Chloe Kelly were among their star performers, while

Jamaican goal ace Khadija 'Bunny' Shaw led the line.

Bunny's childhood nickname – earned thanks to her love of crunching on carrots – had somehow just stuck. Last season she'd scored an amazing thirty-one goals in thirty games, destroying defences in the league and the cups. Despite all her goals, though, Bunny was yet to win a trophy with Manchester City. She was desperate to give the fans something to celebrate.

Bunny had an injury niggle for City's opener in the WSL – a 2–0 victory over West Ham United – but she did make the bench for the next match – a huge clash against Chelsea.

At the sunny Joie Stadium, City's fans were treated to an early goal. Chloe's long-range strike from outside the box was just fabulous! Bunny wished she were on the pitch to perform their celebration dance together!

So far so good – City looked in control. Chelsea, with Lauren James playing wide on the right, hadn't really tested City's teenage keeper, Khiara Keating. Then – disaster! The ref decided that skipper Alex had spent too long taking a free kick and showed her a second yellow card for timewasting. Furious boos rang around the stadium as the half-time whistle blew.

Playing forty-five minutes with only ten players would be tough against any team, but against mighty champions Chelsea? It would take a super-human effort to stop them scoring, and so City played deeper, hoping Chelsea wouldn't unlock their defence.

Then Lauren tried her luck, unleashing a left-footed curler from twenty-five yards. Khiara stood helpless in goal, but the shot rattled back off the bar. So close!

'We need you on that pitch!' City boss Gareth Taylor told Bunny.

So Bunny came off the subs bench, as more chaos followed. Lauren Hemp's pull on LJ earned her a second yellow, just like Alex! Now down to nine players, City would need a miracle to stay in the game. If only Bunny could sneak another goal – she was getting into good positions, but she just couldn't finish her chances.

Chelsea threw the kitchen sink at City after that, even pushing Millie up front as an extra striker. Khiara continued her calm catches, before the bar saved City again in added time.

Then at last the Chelsea goal did come. Guro grabbed it in the ninety-sixth minute. City were gutted! And still the match went on at a frantic pace. Could Chelsea go on and win it? No! Guro and Sam Kerr both fired wide.

'Not a second too soon!' cried Bunny, delighted to hear the final whistle.

What a match! If this was how every match in the WSL would be played, it was set to be an incredible season.

After four games, Chelsea remained unbeaten. Apart from the draw at City, the Blues had earned maximum points. Then on the 4th of November, fireworks came a day early! An unstoppable Chelsea travelled to Aston Villa and hit the home side for six.

But the 6–0 scoreline wasn't what grabbed the headlines that evening. After the match, Emma Hayes gathered her squad in the dressing room, while the players who hadn't travelled to Villa Park – included an injured Lauren – joined a video call to hear what their boss had to say.

Then, with tears in her eyes, Emma made an announcement that sent shockwaves through the world of women's football. At the end of the season, she was quitting Chelsea to take up a new job coaching the United States women's national team.

'We've got one last season together,' Emma told her squad. 'Let's make it count.'

The Chelsea players were devastated, and the news made Lauren drop her phone. Since joining the club, Emma had been like a mum to her. Always there to offer advice and call out the bullies on social media, Emma had Lauren's back even when she didn't deserve it.

This can't be happening, Lauren gasped. It felt like a bad dream.

That night, Lauren made a promise to herself. She would do everything she could on the pitch to pay back Emma's faith in her, and together with her teammates, they would fight for all four trophies.

Following Chelsea's goal-fest, Manchester City's next destination was Arsenal's Meadow Park a day later. By now, Bunny was back in the starting line-up and was relishing the chance to add to her goals tally. City topped the table, but only on goal difference.

Arsenal struck first, but missed a glorious chance to double their lead when City's keeper Khiara pushed Kim Little's penalty onto the post. Save! Then it was Bunny's turn to hit the woodwork, with a diving header.

'Great effort!' Gareth Taylor called from the sidelines. 'Stay focused.'

And that's just what Bunny did next. With her back to goal, she was completely blocked. So instead, Bunny passed to Chloe, who calmly slotted home. 1–1!

'No need to thank me!' Bunny joked.

With just minutes to go, though, there was trouble for City. When Arsenal's Katie McCabe hit a high ball, Khiara rushed out of her box with her arms raised. If she handled the ball, she'd be sent off! She watched helplessly as it bounced over her head. Stina Blackstenius latched on to the pass and claimed a smash-and-grab winner for Arsenal. An awful moment for the young keeper!

City's slip-up saw Chelsea edge ahead in the title race, but it was still early days. Plenty of points were there to be won and lost between now and the end of the season.

Back in the squad after the Villa victory, Lauren made good on her promise of playing for her manager. Her first Chelsea hat-trick came against Liverpool in a rout at the Bridge, and was followed by two goals against Leicester City. No wonder Lauren was voted Women's Super League Player of the Month for November – she had been unbeatable!

CHAPTER 2

WINTER WINS

In December, it was Chelsea's turn to play Arsenal, before a record WSL crowd at Emirates Stadium. The Gunners had tens of thousands more supporters than Chelsea, but that didn't bother Lauren. She dreamed of playing in games like these! With a rocking stadium, and thousands more fans watching on TV, Lauren was buzzing with excitement.

In another life, Lauren might have been lining up for the Gunners, the club where she had made her debut as a sixteen-year-old. Instead, she had moved to Manchester United, before Emma brought her to Chelsea while still a teenager. Now, she was a Blue through and through.

Arsenal made an electric start, with a Beth Mead

belter that had their fans on their feet. But Chelsea soon fought back, when Johanna Rytting Kaneryd fired in the equaliser against the run of play. Before half-time, though, Arsenal scored not once, but twice more to head into the break with a comfortable cushion. With no Millie Bright, out injured, Chelsea's defence was looking seriously shaky.

The second half was more miserable still. Lauren began to feel frustrated in midfield. In the seventieth minute, she gave away a foul. When Arsenal's Lia Wälti went to collect the ball, a red mist came down and Lauren stood on Lia's foot on purpose. Of course, the ref spotted it, with Lauren lucky to only see yellow.

The next minute, Chelsea gave away a penalty that Alessia Russo buried to make it 4–1.

Emma pulled Lauren off the pitch, before things could go from terrible to even worse.

'What were you thinking?' the manager raged. 'You could have really hurt her.'

'Sorry,' said Lauren sulkily. But it was only much later when Lauren realised that she really meant it.

The defeat saw Chelsea's unbeaten run end with a

thud. Now Arsenal moved level on points with Chelsea at the top of the table – three teams were vying to become WSL champions!

Emma was furious with her players, who only had themselves to blame for such a sloppy performance. 'If we want to be champions again, we're going to have to pull our socks up.' But as she reminded them, 'We've lost three points – we haven't lost the title.'

Manchester City, meanwhile, had been hitting fine form. In November, Bunny hit a hat-trick in a sensational 7–0 victory over Spurs that had the Joie Stadium jumping!

'Feed the Bun and she will score!' the fans cried out, cheering on their Jamaican striker.

Then in City's last game before the winter break, Bunny netted three times once again! Even seeing her penalty saved didn't dent Bunny's confidence. Instead, she broke the deadlock with the cheekiest of chips over Everton keeper Courtney Brosnan.

'Love that!' cried Chloe Kelly, jumping into Bunny's arms.

And after completing her hat-trick with a long-range strike and a powerful header, the striker had another match ball to add to her collection!

That made it nine goals in nine games, making Bunny December's Player of the Month and the league's top scorer. What a season it had been so far!

She felt proud of her goals, of course, but winning the Golden Boot wasn't top of her Christmas list; Bunny had her eyes on an even bigger prize – the WSL trophy. City were playing some of their best football, with their team spirit growing stronger every match. And with Chelsea only three points ahead, it was all to play for.

So as the league began its winter break, the table showed three talented teams in the running to become WSL champions.

Pos	Team Name	Played	Wins	Draws	Losses	Goal Diff.	Points
1	Chelsea Women	10	8	1	1	21	25
2	Manchester City Women	10	7	1	2	19	22
3	Arsenal Women	10	7	1	2	14	22

To escape England's freezing temperatures, Chelsea flew to Morocco for some warm-weather training. The camp was supposed to give their players a boost, but sadly, their super striker and stand-in skipper Sam Kerr suffered a bad knee injury that would end her season.

'Nooo!' cried Lauren. She felt desperate for her teammate. 'We'll be with you every step of the way.'

With both Sam and Millie now both nursing knee injuries, Chelsea would have to choose another new captain. It was decided that Erin Cuthbert and Niamh Charles, two brilliant young players, would share the armband.

Right, Lauren decided. *It's time to step things up a gear.* It didn't matter that she was one of the youngest players in the squad – if Chelsea wanted to keep hold of their league title, she was going to have to put in some of the biggest performances of her life. That work began with a game at home to Manchester United.

Stamford Bridge had always been a happy hunting ground for Lauren. Even with Mary Earps, the world's number one goalkeeper standing in her way, the forward felt fearless.

Mary's good, but she's not unbeatable, Lauren said to herself.

Sure enough, just five minutes after kick-off, Lauren guided the ball with the outside of her right boot past Mary in goal. Advantage Chelsea! Soon after, Lauren doubled her team's lead, controlling a Nathalie Björn pass over the top before finishing first time.

'Lauren James loves playing at Stamford Bridge,' said Farah Williams on comms. 'When she's here, you're guaranteed a goal!'

After that, Chelsea eased off the gas a little and let Manchester United pull a goal back. And even after Emma's half-time warning, the visitors continued creating chances. Chelsea had their young keeper Hannah Hampton to thank for keeping them ahead.

Then late on, Lauren saw her chance to score a hat-trick and took it. Sjoeke Nüsken's through-ball fell perfectly as Lauren held off her marker and coolly slotted home. That silenced the Manchester United boos!

Some 20,000 Blues fans were on their feet. Lauren ran to greet some of them behind the goal, high fiving everyone who'd stuck out a hand.

'I think you enjoyed that!' Emma said to Lauren at full-time.

Lauren certainly had! Ever since she was a tiny girl with a football at her feet, she'd dreamed of moments like these.

When a double at Brighton followed next match, Lauren was crowned January's Player of the Month. She'd scored the goals to keep Chelsea top, while City and Arsenal snapped at their heels.

CHAPTER 3

THE QUEST FOR THE QUADRUPLE

As well as leading the league, Chelsea's gutsy performances in the Women's Champions League saw them win their group, taking them through to the final eight teams. Plus, they were still in the FA and League Cups. Fighting for four trophies wouldn't be easy – it would mean playing more matches than any of their rivals. But if they won the lot, this team would go down in history!

Manager Emma, though, never let her side get carried away. 'We'll take one game at a time and see where we are at the end of the season,' she told her squad of superstars.

With Sam Kerr ruled out for the season, January also saw a new striker joining the club. Lauren knew how much of a handful Mayra Ramírez could be from the World Cup. Myra had shone for Colombia in their quarter-final against England. She hoped her new teammate could hit the ground running, as next up was a top-of-the-table clash with Manchester City under the Friday-night lights.

Chelsea hadn't lost at home in the league for more than three years, but it was City who scored first. The goalscorer? Who else but the brilliant Bunny Shaw – poking home with the outside of her boot. She cupped her hand to her ear in celebration before the ball had even crossed the line!

'COME ON, CHELSEA! COME ON, CHELSEA! COME ON, CHELSEA!' the home fans urged.

Mayra, meanwhile, was causing the City defence all sorts of problems. Tripped by Alex Greenwood in the box, the ref signalled to play on. Unlucky!

'Keep going!' Emma shouted from the sidelines.

But no matter how hard they worked, or how many shots they took, Chelsea couldn't get past City's keeper,

Khiara, and slipped to their second defeat of the season. This was serious – no team had been defeated three times and gone on to win the league. Chelsea had now lost twice.

With eight league games left to play, Chelsea and Manchester City had the same number of points and the exact same goal difference too. Predicting the champions was too close to call! The next few months would be all about which team could keep their cool and their players fit.

Only a couple of weeks later, the two teams met again, in the League Cup semi-final. Chelsea wasted no time in getting their revenge and flew out from the kick-off. Mayra slid a pass wide to Lauren, whose shot deflected through Alex's legs and past Khiara in goal.

'Not the prettiest, but they all count!' Lauren breathed a sigh of relief.

And when Alex was denied a late penalty, Lauren's goal turned out to be the winner. Chelsea were thrilled to have reached their first cup final of the season, but it had come at a cost. Now Mayra and Guro were the latest patients on the physio's treatment table.

Both teams were back in action a few days later, in the FA Cup quarter-finals. Chelsea went to Everton, while City headed south to take on Tottenham.

Lauren was sharing the bench with Catarina Macario, who had impressed with a goal on her Chelsea debut, after almost two years out with an ACL injury. Cat was a classy player who could chip in with goals from anywhere across the forward line. Lauren was excited to play with her.

Then came their chance to shine, in a triple substitution with Melanie Leupolz. Emma's tactics proved spot on – it took Cat just three minutes to score the matchwinner. Aggie Beever-Jones put the chance on a plate for Cat to gobble up!

'Great goal!' Lauren said to Cat in the celebrations.

So Chelsea marched on in four competitions.

Meanwhile, in City's quarter-final, luck hadn't been on their side. Some lovely play between Bunny and Mary Fowler had given the Cityzens a dream start. The goal had looked like taking City through, but Spurs' Bethany England pounced to level the match after a mix-up at the back in the ninety-sixth minute. A goalless half-hour of extra time was played out, which meant penalties would decide the semi-finalists. And sadly for City, Spurs scored one more spot-kick to clinch the win.

What a nightmare few days! Knocked out of both cups, the WSL would be City's last chance of silverware. Their league form wasn't in question – City had won every game since a narrow defeat to Brighton back in November, scoring goal after goal. Next, they faced the Seagulls again.

This time, City were solid. Lauren Hemp prodded in their first, before Mary joined her on the scoresheet. But it was City's third goal that got the loudest cheers of the day – Yui Hasegawa crossed to Bunny at the back post, who buried her header. An easy finish in the end, it was a goal that Bunny would never forget. Her sixty-seventh strike since joining the club matched Georgia Stanway's record goals tally! With ten WSL wins in a row, City were flying sky-high!

Chelsea's game that weekend was full of surprises. Arsenal were the visitors at Stamford Bridge, which usually made for a tight contest. But when they arrived, Arsenal's kit man made an embarrassing discovery – he had packed the wrong colour socks!

With no time to beat the London traffic and fetch more, Arsenal had to buy all their players black away socks from the Chelsea gift shop! Then they got busy taping over the Chelsea badge.

The DJ fired up the crowd during the delay until the atmosphere inside the ground was pumping. After surviving a couple of early Arsenal chances, Chelsea began to move through the gears. First to every ball, they pressed all over the pitch. When their first clear-cut chance fell to Lauren, she danced around the Arsenal defence and looped the ball over Manuela Zinsberger. The keeper might have kept it out, but Lauren's shot proved too hot to handle! A knee slide followed. Chelsea's Number 10 had now scored eight goals in just four games at Stamford Bridge. Wow!

And Chelsea fans were cheering again when Sjoeke flicked in Erin's strike from outside the box. At 2–0 down after twenty-one minutes, Arsenal looked shell-shocked! Sjoeke added a third goal soon after, to land the Gunners in deep trouble.

A triple substitution at half-time did little to get Arsenal back into the game. Chelsea were playing with the freedom and confidence that showed exactly why they were the current champions. Even when Arsenal scored a late goal from a lucky deflection, nothing could spoil Chelsea's party spirit.

A fist pump from Emma at the final whistle followed.

The loudest cheers came from Chelsea's injured players, Millie and Sam, the first to invade the pitch. They couldn't have been prouder of their teammates.

'We really socked it to them!' Emma joked in the Chelsea huddle. 'You are all amazing.'

A massive three points in the bag, and Chelsea's title ambitions were clear. It had been the perfect reply to that awful Arsenal defeat in December, which the Chelsea players hadn't let themselves forget.

Erin, on skipper duties, explained Chelsea's attitude best in a post-match interview. 'We have a great way of picking ourselves up – "The Chelsea Way", we call it. When everyone thinks we're down and out, we always find a way.'

Back in European action next, Chelsea looked strong in their double-header against Ajax. Lauren scored away in Amsterdam to set the Blues on their way to a 4–1 victory over two legs.

Now Chelsea were top of the league, were Champions League and FA Cup semi-finalists, and had the League Cup final to play too. They hadn't played sparkling football in every match, but they were still in the hunt for all four trophies.

Lauren smiled. She loved being a part of this team. Even with important players injured, they kept grinding out the wins. And while no one dared whisper it, the dream – of winning a historic quadruple – was getting closer and closer.

CHAPTER 4

TIGHT AT THE TOP

For each team, just six WSL games remained. Things couldn't have been tighter at the top – Chelsea led City only on goal difference. In third place, Arsenal lagged six points behind.

Things were hotting up in the goal-scoring charts too:

Khadija 'Bunny' Shaw:	16 goals
Lauren James:	13 goals

Both teams were going to need their top scorers in the form of their lives for the run-in.

An epic Manchester derby at City's main stadium, the Etihad, was up next. Forty thousand tickets had been sold for the match, and Bunny couldn't wait to take centre stage.

'Whenever we play United it's always a big game,' she buzzed to the television cameras. 'We need to keep the momentum going and hopefully we can get the job done.'

She thought back with a smile to the last time the teams had met in the league at Old Trafford. City had left United as red-faced as their shirts!

United had led through a penalty, before City had replied with two quick-fire goals. In the second half, a chance had fallen to Bunny. When Maya Le Tissier had hit a poor back-pass to Mary Earps, it was fifty-fifty as to who would reach the ball first – Bunny or Mary.

I'm just going to go for it! Bunny had bravely flown into the tackle.

With Mary bearing down on her at full speed, the ball had cannoned off Bunny's right boot and into the back of the net! Thanks to Bunny's perfect pressing: 3–1. Manchester was sky blue that day!

Now, could Bunny do it all over again? After a slow start, City were growing into the game. Young attacker

Jess Park scored twice, before creating a lovely assist for Bunny. When the ball slipped expertly into her path, Bunny left Maya for dust and struck the ball into the bottom right corner of the goal. What a way to become City's all-time leading scorer in the WSL! The win placed City top – at least until Chelsea played the next day.

After the game, Bunny was as humble as always. 'Of course, the girls look for me to score,' she told the journalists. 'It's not easy, but I just try to do the best that I can.'

West Ham United, meanwhile, proved a tougher opposition than Chelsea might have liked. Although the Blues led through Aggie's early strike, they didn't score again until Erin blasted home a thunderbolt two minutes from time. A scrappy performance, but Lauren and her teammates didn't mind – all that mattered were the three points.

Next, Chelsea's attentions turned to the cups. They had not one, but two huge knockout matches to play, with the League Cup final against Arsenal and an FA Cup semi-final away to Manchester United still to come.

Sadly, Chelsea would taste defeat against Arsenal, who delivered the knockout goal in extra time. Meanwhile, in the FA Cup, Chelsea were left stunned when Manchester United raced into a 2–0 lead halfway through the first half. And despite Lauren pulling a goal back for Chelsea, United held on to finally beat the Blues for the first time.

So, the quadruple wasn't to be. Lauren and her teammates were disappointed, of course, but they were determined to come back even stronger. There were still the WSL and the Champions League trophies to fight for, with the players desperate to deliver both titles for Emma. They couldn't leave their beloved coach empty-handed in her final season as Chelsea boss! Could Chelsea find their form again and put their two cup exits firmly behind them, or would they crumble completely under the pressure?

Emma had a plan. When Chelsea were back in action facing Aston Villa, she made seven changes from the Manchester United defeat. Chelsea's big names dropped to the bench, while a poorly Lauren was rested completely. It was a risky plan, but one that worked perfectly – the Blues bounced back, scoring three good goals, while Hannah kept a clean sheet.

Now the team would be fresh for their biggest matches of the season: two Champions League matches against the current champions and best club side in the world, Barcelona.

Chelsea flew to Spain with a game plan. The two teams had met in the competition twice before, with Barcelona shattering Chelsea hearts both times. This time, the Blues would try to snuff out Barça's attacks and mark their creative players, including Aitana Bonmatí, Caroline Graham Hansen and Salma Paralluelo, out of the game.

As the teams lined up in the Olimpic Lluis Companys stadium, Chelsea faced an uphill battle – Barcelona hadn't lost at home since 2019!

'Unbeaten runs are there to be beaten,' captain Erin told her team with a confident smile. 'Let's show this lot what we can do!'

The way to win would be to concentrate on the positives – not only was Lauren back in the eleven, but Millie was on the bench for the first time in months!

After a shaky start, Chelsea began to settle down. Barça had most of the ball, but Chelsea looked dangerous on the break. Then when a chance fell to Erin, after good work from Sjoeke, she smashed her shot past Cata Coll in goal. *BANG!*

Lauren raced over to give her a hug. 'What a hit!' she gasped.

'I've been watching you in training!' Erin joked modestly.

The match continued with Chelsea's backline working tirelessly to break down Barcelona's attacks. It was going to plan until midway through the second half, when – *PEEEEP!* – the ref blew for a handball in Chelsea's box. Penalty against Kadeisha Buchanan!

Nooooo! thought Lauren. There was nothing Kadeisha could have done. Her heart sank.

A long VAR check followed before the ref signalled again. No penalty! Salma had been offside in the build-up. Thank goodness!

Shortly after, Lauren looked to the bench. Still battling a heavy cold, she couldn't finish the match. On went Cat.

More chances fell Barcelona's way next, but Salma and Alexia Putellas unbelievably missed the target from close range. When the final whistle blew, Chelsea celebrated a famous victory: 1–0! They were halfway to the Champions League final in Bilbao!

But as everyone knows, football is a game of two halves. A record home crowd of almost forty thousand fans streamed into Stamford Bridge for the return leg, Emma's final match at the Bridge. She had been Chelsea boss for twelve long years, during which time she had taken the club from being second from bottom of the WSL, right to the top.

Her record as manager spoke for itself: with six league titles, five FA Cups and two League Cups, Emma had moulded Chelsea into a winning machine. The one trophy that had always escaped her was the big one – the Champions League. Could her players give her the fairy-tale ending she craved?

Lauren desperately wanted to play, but nervous energy had begun to swirl in her stomach. She phoned Emma the night before the match.

'It's 11 o'clock at night!' Emma moaned. Her head

had already hit the pillow! 'I'll tell you what I tell my little boy, Harry – you'll be grumpy in the morning!'

'It's about the match . . .' Lauren began. 'I don't think I'll be ready.'

Emma sighed. She knew that Lauren had been feeling poorly all week, that she'd only been able to take part in one training session. Her players' health came first, of course, but Emma suspected that something more than a cold was bothering Lauren.

'I'll put you on the bench if that's what you want,' Emma said. 'But do you really want to miss out on playing the best team in the world at Stamford Bridge?'

'But Boss, what if I let you all down?' Lauren worried.

'Or what if you win us the match? Get some sleep, Lauren,' Emma said softly, before hanging up.

Emma always knew the right words to make Lauren feel better. And by the time the teams walked out of the tunnel at Stamford Bridge, Lauren's worries had melted away.

Even so, Barcelona seemed to have all the luck in the second leg. Aitana showed why she was voted the world's best player, sending Niamh spinning before her deflected shot flew beyond Hannah's dive. Fluky!

The goal sparked Lauren into action. She fired a cut-back to Melanie Leupolz with the goal gaping. Melanie got the shot away, but the ball bounced back off the bar. Miss!

In the second half, Barcelona got luckier still. Kadeisha was shown a second yellow card for a challenge on Patri Guijarro.

'No way was that a yellow!' Lauren cried, but the ref wasn't budging. Kadeisha was off!

Next Barcelona won a penalty, when Aitana went down easily in the box. The Chelsea crowd did their best to put off Fridolina Rolfö, but the winger sent Hannah the wrong way. Now Barcelona were ahead in the tie.

'Noooo!' cried Lauren, screwing up her face. It seemed such an unfair way to go behind.

Emma made a triple substitution for one last throw of the dice. Millie was thrown up front as an emergency striker, while Lauren's legs had nothing left to give – and off she came.

Sadly, Chelsea couldn't find a way to score. Their Champions League dream had ended in deep disappointment.

The Chelsea players were heartbroken. They had given absolutely everything to try and win the trophy for Emma, and to come closer to beating Barcelona than ever before.

The next day at training, the pain of their defeat slowly began to sting a little less. Millie gathered the squad for a team talk.

'We're all gutted about last night,' she began. 'But we are Chelsea – we never give up. We have one trophy left to fight for, so let's bring it home!'

Everyone cheered and clapped. What did Emma call her players? Mentality monsters! They could always find the courage and strength to battle back from disappointment. That's what made them winners.

CHAPTER 5

A ROLLERCOASTER RUN-IN

But Chelsea were no longer top of the league. Manchester City had been on a winning streak since November and were now three points and three goals ahead of them, although they had played one game more.

Playing so many matches in a short space of time had taken its toll on Lauren. Now she had an annoying foot injury. The fans were worried – how bad was it? As usual, Emma was playing her cards close to her chest, and refused to say when her Number 10 might be fit again. All Lauren could do now was to rest and work on her physio exercises, hoping to be back for the final few games.

The Blues' next match, away to Liverpool, came too soon for Lauren, who could only watch events unfold on TV back in London. It was a game that turned the title race on its head.

Chelsea started on the front foot when Aggie, unmarked, nodded home a header from a corner. But Liverpool replied with a copycat goal just after the restart. The Reds took the lead next, only for Aggie to reply with a fierce volley for 2–2. After their European exploits a few days earlier, Chelsea were tiring, but they weren't giving up.

Just a minute later, Liverpool led again, scoring from a quick counter-attack. With nine minutes, plus added time, to go – could Chelsea fight back?

Yes! Cat's shot was turned in by the keeper for an own goal. The action was end-to-end! But in added time, Gemma Bonner's towering header won it for Liverpool. Chelsea were sunk! If City won their final two games, they would be champions. Chelsea couldn't catch them.

'The title is done,' Emma told the TV cameras.

Tears flowed out from the players in Blue. They just

couldn't see a way back.

City meanwhile had been dealt a major blow to their own title hopes. After scoring twice, Bunny had limped off in their win over West Ham.

'How is she?' coach Gareth Taylor asked the physios after the match.

They shook their heads. 'It's not looking good.'

An x-ray confirmed that Bunny had broken a bone in her foot. An injury that would take months to heal. It was the worst timing ever – she had been scoring for fun. Her twenty-one goals in the WSL put her well ahead of Lauren James in the race for the Golden Boot. If City were going to win the league, they would have to do it without their star striker.

City were glad to be playing at home next, but it was another big occasion. Their opponents Arsenal still had a chance to finish as runners-up and would be no pushover.

At the Joie Stadium, the fans had come out in force see their side edge closer to the title, as well as to say goodbye to City legend Steph Houghton, who was hanging up her boots at the end of the season.

Fireworks blasted and music blared before kick-off. It was set to be an emotional day!

Lauren Hemp, outstanding all season, put City ahead with a super strike. She ran straight to the subs' bench for a hug with Steph.

'Great stuff,' said Steph. 'We've got this!'

City kept toiling away, but Arsenal were not giving up. It took until the ninetieth minute for the Gunners to score, but score they did – Stina Blackstenius netting after a goalmouth scramble. Then in stoppage time Stina stole all three points for Arsenal, scoring her second of a dramatic double. What a sucker punch!

Lauren was watching the match on TV when her phone buzzed. It was Emma asking whether her injured player was coming to watch their match against Bristol City.

'I'll be there,' Lauren promised. 'But have you seen the score?'

Emma hadn't. She was driving to Kingsmeadow. 'Are you going to tell me then, or what?' she asked, desperate for news.

'Hang on . . .' said Lauren. A long pause followed.

'Yes, they've done it. Arsenal have won!'

Emma gasped. 'You're a great player, LJ, but you'd make a terrible commentator!'

With the title race blown open again, Chelsea saw their opportunity. Maybe, just maybe . . .

If they were going to have any chance at all, they would have to win. And win BIG. It was time to believe.

Their fans at Kingsmeadow were in full voice.

Flying high, up in the sky,
We'll keep the blue flag flying high,
From Kingsmeadow to Wemb-er-ley,
We'll keep the blue flag flying high!

Guro gave Chelsea a golden start, a penalty after six minutes. 1–0.

Sjoeke scrambled in the second goal from a corner.

Aggie fired in after a one-two with Erin.

Guro grabbed her second, thumping her Chelsea badge in celebration. It was already 4–0 . . . and then she finished at the near post for her hat-trick.

Niamh steered home a set piece for number six,

before Guro scored an amazing fourth to put Chelsea in seventh heaven.

'We want eight!' chanted the Chelsea crowd, and that's exactly what they got. Aggie delivered with a stooping header. 8–0!

Emma couldn't stop smiling. What an incredible bunch of players these girls were. It felt bitter-sweet to be leaving them. Chelsea were still three points behind City, but their enormous win meant their goal difference was now better. A win against Spurs next would see the title decided on the final day of the season.

The game at Tottenham was tense and tight, with a single goal scored this time. Thankfully, it went to Chelsea – forward Maika Hamano's first Blues strike the winner. And there was more good news – Lauren was back! Coming off the subs' bench felt incredible.

Chelsea were now table-toppers again with a two-goal advantage over City with just one game each to play.

The final fixtures were Aston Villa v Manchester City, and Manchester United v Chelsea.

On paper, Chelsea had a trickier tie. They had to take on the newly crowned FA Cup winners at Old Trafford. But something had shifted in the Chelsea players' minds. Their tears had long since dried, while their nerves were steeled for battle.

Lauren made the bench again, as Mayra went straight back into the starting line-up. The Colombian had barely trained in weeks, but was desperate to be Chelsea's secret weapon.

And – *BOOM!* – within two minutes, Mayra had out-muscled Millie Turner and planted her header past Mary Earps. Exactly the start Chelsea had wanted!

Next, Mayra slid a pass to Johanna Rytting Kaneryd who made it 2–0 after eight minutes. Afterwards she bombed down the wing and delivered a perfect pass into the box – Sjoeke couldn't miss. And Mayra wasn't stopping there – she powered past two defenders and smashed the ball into the back of the net. It was 4–0 for Chelsea at the break, and Manchester United's defence was missing in action!

The news was trickling through to the City fans at Villa Park. City were in front there too, but were now a massive five goals behind Chelsea.

A further forty-five minutes of hard work, concentration and self-belief followed at Old Trafford. Melanie Leupolz and Super Fran Kirby rounded off a special performance: 6–0. Chelsea had crushed United. Against the odds, they had found a way to become WSL champions for a record fifth time in a row!

Then came the celebrations. Champagne sprayed the players on the podium, fireworks exploded, and golden ticker tape rained down. Millie and Emma lifted the trophy together in a perfect moment.

Lauren clutched her medal close to her chest – the medal she had fought so hard to win. It had been a special season, the best of her life, but she would be ready to chase more trophies with Chelsea when the time came. She just loved the club!

As for Bunny, she had not one but two of her own trophies to lift for her unbelievable performances in a sky-blue shirt. The WSL Golden Boot and Player of the Season awards both belonged to Bunny!

Two top players at two classy clubs. Bunny and Lauren couldn't wait to go again next season.

WOMEN'S SUPER LEAGUE FINAL TABLE							
Pos	Team Name	Played	Wins	Draws	Losses	Goal Diff.	Points
1	**Chelsea**	**22**	**18**	**1**	**3**	**53**	**55**
2	Manchester City	22	18	1	3	46	55
3	Arsenal	22	16	2	4	33	50
4	Liverpool	22	12	5	5	8	41
5	Manchester United	22	10	5	7	10	35
6	Tottenham	22	8	7	7	-5	31
7	Aston Villa	22	7	3	12	-16	24
8	Everton	22	6	5	11	-13	23
9	Brighton & Hove Albion	22	5	4	13	-22	19
10	Leicester City	22	4	6	12	-19	18
11	West Ham	22	3	6	13	-25	15
12	*Bristol City*	*22*	*1*	*3*	*18*	*-50*	*6*

WOMEN'S SUPER LEAGUE TOP SCORERS				
		Goals	Assists	Games
1	Khadija Shaw	21	3	18
2=	Lauren James	13	2	16
2=	Elisabeth Terland	13	1	22
4	Alessia Russo	12	4	22
5=	Lauren Hemp	11	8	21
5=	Agnes Beever-Jones	11	2	17
7	Amalie Thestrup	9	0	22
8=	Beth Mead	8	4	20
8=	Sjoeke Nüsken	8	3	21
8=	Nikita Parris	8	1	21
8=	Rachel Daly	8	0	20

TOP 5 TEAM PERFORMANCES

On some days, everything just clicks. Goalkeepers seem unbeatable, defences solid, midfielders creative and attackers clinical. And when that happens in the most important games, it leads to incredible performances. Just like in these five games . . .

1 BARCELONA FEMENÍ 0–1 CHELSEA WOMEN

Before Chelsea arrived, Barcelona hadn't lost a competitive match at home since February 2019. That's more than half a decade! Yet a sensational defensive display from Emma Hayes's side secured a 1–0 victory in this Champions League semi-final first leg thanks to a winner from Erin Cuthbert. Using a back five, Chelsea limited Barcelona's attacking threat so much that their first shot on target came only in second half injury time. And using a dynamic counter-attack, Chelsea carried plenty of threat themselves. A tactical masterclass from Emma Hayes in her final season at the club.

2 ARSENAL 1–0 MANCHESTER CITY

Arsenal may have beaten Manchester City on penalties in the Community Shield to kickstart the season, but many still wondered if Mikel Arteta's team could perform when it truly mattered. It had been almost eight years since Arsenal's last Premier League victory over City. Yet this determined, disciplined display not only changed that run, but also proved Arsenal were true title contenders.

It wasn't pretty. There wasn't a lot of beautiful football on display. But Arteta's careful organisation limited City to just four shots, and his substitutions worked to perfection as the fresh Kai Havertz teed up the fresh Gabriel Martinelli to bag a dramatic late winner for the Gunners.

3 LEVERKUSEN 3–0 BAYERN

Gary Lineker once said 'Football is a simple game. 22 people chase a ball for 90 minutes and at the end, the Germans always win.' Yet in Germany, the truth is a little different. Because in Germany, Bayern Munich *always* win.

The Bundesliga has been dominated by the Bavarians. After winning eleven league titles in a row they were in pursuit of a twelfth. There was just one problem: Bayer Leverkusen. Xabi Alonso's side had come from nowhere to push them all the way. And with this performance, Leverkusen moved five points clear at the top of the table.

So dominant were Leverkusen that Bayern Munich managed just a single shot on target. Winger Leroy Sané was so angry that he punched a camera! The German giants couldn't deal with Bayer Leverkusen's rampaging wing-backs. Nor their 3-4-3 formation. Nor their high-risk, high-reward football, which would later be *really* rewarded.

4 SHEFFIELD UNITED 0–8 NEWCASTLE UNITED

Scintillating. Sparkling. Simply unstoppable. Newcastle United equalled their biggest ever Premier League win with an irresistible away performance against struggling Sheffield United.

Yet Newcastle didn't actually start the game amazingly well. Having lost three of their opening five league games, they appeared sluggish in this early season contest. Until the introduction, twelve minutes in, of Anthony Gordon, whose pace and energy lifted his team instantly. It was Gordon who created the first goal after twenty-one minutes from a cutback. And after that, the floodgates opened.

Sheffield United didn't know what to do! Gordon was proving a nightmare for their defenders, but so too were Kieran Trippier's set-pieces. On three occasions, Trippier's deliveries ended in goals for Newcastle, whose eight goals in total came from eight different goalscorers! Newcastle's entire team tore Sheffield United apart, creating chances at will, and their eight goals were no less than they deserved.

5 MANCHESTER UNITED WOMEN 0–6 CHELSEA

After twenty-one games, the WSL title was decided on one dramatic final day. Chelsea and Manchester City shared the same number of points, but Chelsea had a better goal difference by two. Chelsea, who had looked out of the race after their defeat to Liverpool, had a slight advantage thanks to Manchester City's late defeat to Arsenal. But still, they'd need a good performance against a Manchester United side who had won the FA Cup the previous weekend.

For Manchester City the task was simple: they had to beat Aston Villa. And they had to score plenty of goals. Many teams would have crumbled under the pressure. But Chelsea were energised. With superstar Sam Kerr injured, Mayra Ramirez led the line. She was on fire!

It took just two minutes for her to open the scoring with a powerful header. Six minutes later she set up Johanna Rytting Kaneryd. By half-time, with Chelsea 4–0 up, the game was all but over. Emma Hayes's side were quicker, stronger, and better all over the pitch.

Ramirez led by example, charging past opponents with ease. Two further goals followed in the second half. Manchester City, meanwhile, could only win 2–1.

A true champion performance from Chelsea – and the perfect send-off for outgoing manager Emma Hayes!

CHAMPIONS LEAGUE

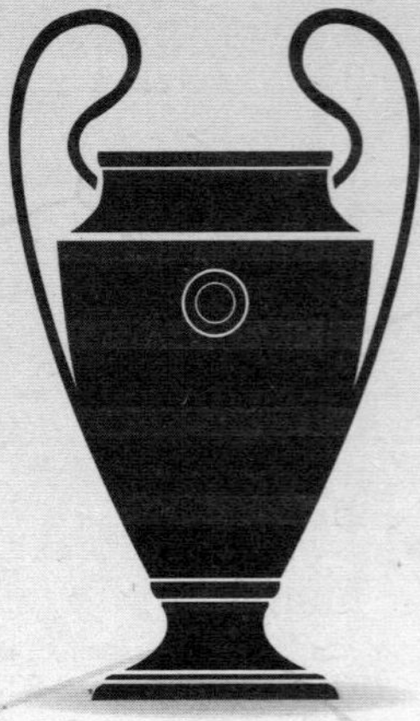

CHAMPIONS LEAGUE REVIEW

"Are you ready to win *La Decimoquinta*?" Toni Kroos asked Jude Bellingham.

"*La Decimo*-what?" Jude replied with a puzzled expression.

"*La Decimoquinta* means the 15th," Toni explained to his English team-mate. "As in a 15th Champions League title – that's our big target for this season."

The pair were chatting at the start of the 2023–24 season, not long after Jude had joined Real Madrid from Borussia Dortmund and was getting to grips with a new environment in a new country.

Fast-forward nine months and Jude knew everything about *La Decimoquinta* – and a lot more Spanish too! By this point, everyone was talking about it as Real needed to win one more match – the Champions

League final against Dortmund at Wembley – to create a new slice of history.

When it came to the Champions League, Real Madrid ruled supreme. They had won the competition 14 times, double the total of the next team on the list, AC Milan. This included five victories in the past ten years alone. What's more, they had played in a quarter of all of the finals since the competition first launched as the European Cup in 1955.

For Toni, the final not only offered a chance to win yet another trophy but also to deliver the perfect ending to his time at Real. It would be the German international's last ever club game before he retired, bringing to an end a glittering career that had begun in 2007 with Bayern Munich.

"You two were barely out of nappies when I made my professional debut," Toni joked with Jude and Vinícius Jr as they prepared for the final.

For Jude, in contrast, the match at Wembley – a stadium he knew very well as an England international – would be the first of what he hoped would be many Champions League finals.

"If I can win even half of what you've achieved in your career, I'll be a happy man," Jude replied to Toni.

"Well, let's make sure you win your first Champions League medal tonight, although it must be strange for you to play against your old Dortmund team-mates," Toni said.

"Yes, I'll have some mixed feelings . . . but I'll definitely want to get one over them!"

On paper, Real Madrid were strongly favoured to get the better of their German opponents. While Dortmund had only managed a fifth-placed finish in the Bundesliga, Madrid's star-studded squad on the other hand had cantered to the La Liga title.

However, anyone watching the first half at Wembley could have been forgiven for thinking that the team in the yellow shirts, not the white of Real, were the dominant force of European football. Quite simply, Dortmund dominated. They created chance after chance but – no matter what they threw at the Spanish side – the ball just would not go in the net.

Julian Brandt side-footed past the post. Karim Adeyemi went clean through on goal but ran too wide. Niclas Füllkrug hit the woodwork. Thibaut Courtois – returning from injury to play his first Champions League match of the season – pulled off two huge saves.

Somehow, Real survived the onslaught and made it through to half-time with the score still at 0–0. A lot of teams might have expected a fiery reception from their manager in the dressing room, but Carlo Ancelotti has always done things differently. Real Madrid's 'Mr Cool' was focusing on the positive side.

"Dortmund have played well, they created some good chances, but – thanks to Thibaut – they haven't taken them," he said with a nod to his keeper.

"Now let's make them pay the price. Remember, boys, we always find a way to win."

As was so often the case, Carlo was right. In the quarter-finals, Real had been outplayed for large parts of their tie against defending champions Manchester City, but refused to give in, eventually sealing victory when Antonio Rüdiger scored the winning penalty in a nerve-racking shootout.

In the semi-final against Bayern Munich, the

situation had felt even more desperate. With 88 minutes on the clock, the Spaniards were heading out of the competition. Yet a matter of minutes later, in a remarkable turnaround, they booked their place at Wembley after Joselu scored two last-gasp goals.

With Carlo's encouragement ringing in their ears, Real were reborn in the second half. Within three minutes of the restart, Toni's vicious free kick forced a save from Gregor Kobel. Soon afterwards, Dani Carvajal called the keeper into action again, then Jude came within centimetres of heading his side into the lead after narrowly failing to connect with Vini's delicious cross.

So impressive in the first half, Dortmund now struggled to stop the Madrid machine and, after 73 minutes, the inevitable breakthrough came.

Just as he had done so many times throughout his glittering career, Toni created the opportunity. The set-piece specialist's corner landed right on the head of Dani, who powered it past the keeper into the far corner.

"Perfect delivery, Toni!" Dani said. "What are we going to do without you?"

"Let's worry about that after we've won this match," Toni replied.

Minutes later, his magic wand of a right foot almost did exactly that. Toni whipped another free kick up and over the wall, only for it to be clawed away by Gregor Kobel.

The Dortmund keeper was performing heroics but, on 82 minutes, was helpless to prevent Real from adding a second. This time it was Toni's young team-mates who did the damage as Jude's pass found Vini in space in the penalty area. The Brazilian did the rest, dinking the ball into the net.

2-0! *La Decimoquinta* was within touching distance.

"Real Madrid is in safe hands with you two in the team," Toni said to Jude and Vini as he joined the goal celebrations.

As the final whistle neared, Carlo gave the chance for the Wembley crowd to show its appreciation for Toni when he substituted him for another Real great, Luka Modrić. As Toni left the pitch and waved to the fans, the stadium roared its support for the German superstar who had once again produced a stellar performance on the biggest stage.

It wasn't long before Toni was back on the pitch, however, joining his team-mates in a lap of honour – and hoisted onto their shoulders – at full-time.

"I've learned so much from you even in just one season," said Jude. "We're going to miss you."

"Not as much as I'll miss all you lot," replied Toni with a smile. "I'll miss winning these medals too."

For Toni, Luka, Dani and team captain Nacho, it was a sixth Champions League medal, equalling the record of Paco Gento, the legendary winger who used to play for – you guessed it! – Real Madrid.

For Carlo, the victory over Dortmund was his fifth Champions League success as a manager, another record. And for Real, a 15th win in this competition further cemented their position as the kings of Europe.

"Anyone know the Spanish for 16?" joked Jude.

INTER	2	PSV EINDHOVEN	1	**PSG**	4	NAPOLI	2
ATLETICO MADRID	2	**BORUSSIA DORTMUND**	3	REAL SOCIEDAD	1	**BARCELONA**	4

ATLETICO MADRID	4	**PSG**	6
BORUSSIA DORTMUND	5	BARCELONA	4

BORUSSIA DORTMUND	2
PSG	0

BORUSSIA DORTMUND	0
REAL MADRID	2

BAYERN MUNICH	3
REAL MADRID	4

ARSENAL	2	REAL MADRID	4
BAYERN MUNICH	3	MAN CITY	4

FC PORTO	1	LAZIO	1	RB LEIPZIG	1	FC COPENHAGEN	2
ARSENAL	1	**BAYERN MUNICH**	3	**REAL MADRID**	2	**MAN CITY**	6

CHAMPIONS LEAGUE TOP SCORERS				
		Goals	Assists	Games
1=	Harry Kane	8	4	12
1=	Kylian Mbappé	8	0	12
3=	Vinícius Júnior	6	4	10
3=	Erling Haaland	6	1	9
3=	Antoine Griezmann	6	1	10
6=	Galeno	5	3	7
6=	Phil Foden	5	3	8
6=	Julián Álvarez	5	2	7
6=	Rodrygo	5	2	13
6=	Álvaro Morata	5	1	10
6=	Joselu	5	0	11
6=	Rasmus Højlund	5	0	6

TOP 5 INDIVIDUAL PERFORMANCES

Difference-makers. Match-winners. Superstar performers. These five players showed up when it mattered most and took the game by the scruff of its neck. Are these 10 out of 10 performances? We think so . . .

1 ADEMOLA LOOKMAN (ATLANTA 3–0 BAYER LEVERKUSEN, EUROPA LEAGUE FINAL)

Lookman was simply unbeatable, scoring all three goals in Atlanta's stunning Europa League final win. He became the first player to ever complete a hat-trick in a Europa League final, and his all-round play deservedly won him the man-of-the-match award.

He opened his account in the twelfth minute after reacting quickest to a square ball. Fourteen minutes later, he curled in a spectacular effort, and then repeated the trick in the seventy-fifth minute.

At times, it felt like Lookman could beat his opponent at will. Sharp throughout, dangerous, and energetic, he ended the hopes of a Leverkusen side of going an entire season unbeaten.

2 COLE PALMER (CHELSEA 6–0 EVERTON, PREMIER LEAGUE)

Even though this game kicked off in April, the temperature soon dipped as 'Cold' Palmer got to work. Having started the season on the bench, there was no doubt that Palmer had by now become the main man. Scoring four goals (including a hat-trick in just sixteen minutes), he blew Everton away with his skill and intelligence.

The pick of the goals was his first, scored after thirteen minutes. He received the ball midway through the Everton half, then nutmegged Everton defender Jarrad Branthwaite before looking up, playing a one-two with striker Nicolas Jackson, andstroking the ball into the corner from twenty yards.

Palmer's third goal wasn't too bad either: a forty-yard lob over Everton keeper Jordan Pickford with his weaker right foot!

He even managed a 'perfect' hat-trick (left foot, right foot, header), before winning and scoring a penalty which took him to the joint top of the race for the Golden Boot with twenty goals.

Cole Palmer FC was on fire once more!

3 KHIARA KEATING (ARSENAL 0–1 MANCHESTER CITY, FA WOMEN'S CUP FIFTH ROUND)

Returning to Meadow Park was not easy for Khiara Keating. In her previous visit she'd lost Manchester City the game with two costly errors. This time round, for the FA Cup fifth round, she was determined to make it up to her team.

No matter what Arsenal threw at her, she was equal to it. There was an incredible tip over the bar, a quick back-pedal to acrobatically claw Victoria Pelova's goal-bound header off the line, a smart reaction to retrieve a corner kick which almost crossed the line. And that was just in second-half stoppage time!

Throughout the match, it wasn't just Keating's shot-stopping that won City the game. She also consistently started dangerous attacks with her pinpoint passing and distribution. It was her fourth clean sheet in a row, and arguably her most impressive. 'A worldie performance,' Arsenal's Caitlin Foord grudgingly said of Keating. Few could argue with that . . .

4 ERLING HAALAND (LUTON 2–6 MANCHESTER CITY, FA CUP FIFTH ROUND)

Erling Haaland means one thing: goals. And in the FA Cup fifth round, he was certainly in the mood for goals.

Supplied by chief creator Kevin De Bruyne, Haaland's powerful shooting boots proved too much for Luton; he bagged an incredible five of them.

In such form, Haaland proved unstoppable. His movement dragged Luton's defence this way and that. His intelligence meant they could never get close to him. And his telepathic link with De Bruyne saw him presented with chance after chance. De Bruyne ended the night with four assists thanks to Haaland's sharp shooting – and Manchester City ended the night one step closer to their attempted 'double treble'.

5 MAYRA RAMIREZ (MANCHESTER UNITED 0–6 CHELSEA, WSL)

Big games need big players to step up. With the WSL title on the line, Ramirez didn't just step up: she soared!

Despite missing the previous four games through injury, she got to work straight away. It took just two minutes for her to open the scoring with a bullet header . . . and she wasn't stopping there. Two goals and two assists later, she'd driven her team to a 6–0 win – and the title. Quicker and stronger than Manchester United, it seemed that nobody was able to stop her. Her second goal summed up her whole performance – she burst past two defenders in the area before thumping a shot past keeper Mary Earps.

With her work done, Ramirez was substituted just before the hour. She'd taken charge of the show and earned her rest with a champion's display.

EUROPA LEAGUE

EUROPA LEAGUE REVIEW

'It's mission impossible,' said Davide Zappacosta.

'No one has beaten Bayer Leverkusen all season,' said Gianluca Scamacca.

'No one has beaten them for a whole year!' added Matteo Ruggeri.

'Well, it's only 361 days, to be precise,' chipped in Ademola Lookman with a chuckle.

It was no laughing matter, of course – Atalanta were getting ready for the biggest match in the northern Italian club's 116-year history. The Europa League final. The chance to win only their second ever trophy – and a first for 61 years.

And if they were to end the trophy drought, they would have to do something that no other side had managed all season: beat Bayer Leverkusen. The newly crowned German champions had enjoyed a simply stunning season, ending Bayern Munich's run of eleven consecutive Bundesliga titles, while also beating anyone who crossed their path in the Europa League, and indeed in the German cup competition, the DFB-Pokal.

Along the way, Leverkusen had built a reputation for not knowing how to lose, time and again scoring late goals to preserve their unbeaten record.

There was no doubt it would take an extraordinary performance from Atalanta to stop the Leverkusen juggernaut, but as the players were discussing the gigantic task facing them that evening, Ademola felt it was important to lighten the mood.

The Nigerian winger recognised – if they were to succeed – that the team needed to have a positive mindset and also to banish any thoughts about the Coppa Italia final they had lost to Juventus only seven days earlier.

After a career that had seen him jump from club to club, including Charlton Athletic, Everton, Fulham and Leicester, plus RB Leipzig in Germany, Ademola knew how lucky he was to play in a European final and was determined to savour the opportunity.

'Let's get out there and enjoy it, boys – it's not every day you get to play in a European final,' he told his teammates in the pre-match huddle. 'Yes, Bayer are a great team . . . but we're pretty good too.'

'Davide, remember we topped our Europa League group without losing a game.'

'Gianluca, remember your goals at Anfield when we shocked Liverpool 3–0.'

'Matteo, don't forget we knocked out a great Marseille side in the semi-final.'

These were exactly the stirring reminders the team needed just before they walked out with their captain Berat Djimsiti, on to the pitch at Dublin's Aviva Stadium. An ear-splitting roar rose from the stands to greet the two sides.

Not only were Atalanta full of belief, but they were also buoyed by the tactical wizardry of their veteran manager, Gian Piero Gasperini, who had been plotting the downfall of the German side.

From the referee's first whistle, the blue-and-black striped Atalanta players swarmed all over the white of Leverkusen, refusing to give their opponents any space or time to play.

In the fifteenth minute, the Italians made a deserved breakthrough. After some slick build-up play down the right wing, Davide's cross found its way to Ademola waiting at the back post. His smart left-foot finish did the rest.

As Ademola turned away in celebration, he was engulfed in hugs from his teammates as well as from some substitutes running on to the pitch. To score in a European final was a special moment, but Ademola knew there was plenty of work to do before they could start celebrating.

'Straight back to business, boys,' he said.

'Go get us another goal, Ademola,' Matteo said.

Ten minutes later, Ademola did just that – and this one was even more magical. He picked up the ball in the middle of the field, thirty-five yards from goal. Running directly at his backtracking opponents, he nutmegged the Leverkusen midfielder Granit Xhaka, flicked the ball onto his right foot and curled it into the far corner from outside the box.

It was a moment of exquisite individual

skill – celebrated with an equally exquisite knee slide.

Even though Atalanta were leading by two goals, Gian Piero stressed to his players at the half-time break that they couldn't take anything for granted. On four previous occasions in the 2023–24 season, Bayer had trailed by two goals, only to fight back every time. That included their last-16 opponents Qarabağ who had been heading into the quarter-finals as the match entered added time, before Leverkusen turned the tie on its head with two quick-fire goals.

'This team will never give up,' Gian Piero said, looking each player in the eye. 'Be prepared for a second-half onslaught – they will throw the kitchen sink at you, plus the fridge and the freezer too.'

Sure enough, as Gian Piero had predicted, Bayer had plenty of possession after half-time but, in a twist from the usual script of 2023–24, they couldn't make it count. The well-organised Atalanta defence could not be breached.

With fifteen minutes remaining, as Leverkusen poured more players forward in a bid to get back into the game, Gianluca launched a quick counter-attack.

Surging into Bayer's half, he found Ademola with a crisp pass. Oozing confidence, the winger bamboozled Edmond Tapsoba with a stepover, switching the ball to his left foot before blasting it into the top corner.

'What. A. Goal!' screamed Davide.

Ademola could barely believe what had just happened. He had only moved to Atalanta a couple of years ago and now he had written his name into club folklore forever!

Unbelievably, it was his first-ever hat-trick in senior football – and he had saved it for the biggest occasion of all. Only five other players had scored a hat-trick in a European final.

And this time, even for Leverkusen's escape artists, there was no coming back. No more last-minute miracles – just an acceptance that, on this occasion, they had been beaten by the better team.

The final whistle confirmed Atalanta's 3–0 win and their first ever European triumph. All that remained was for Berat to raise the famously heavy Europa League trophy – all 15 kilograms of it – in front of his joyous teammates.

Ademola, meanwhile, clutched something equally precious, if a little lighter: the match ball, a precious souvenir for his historic hat-trick.

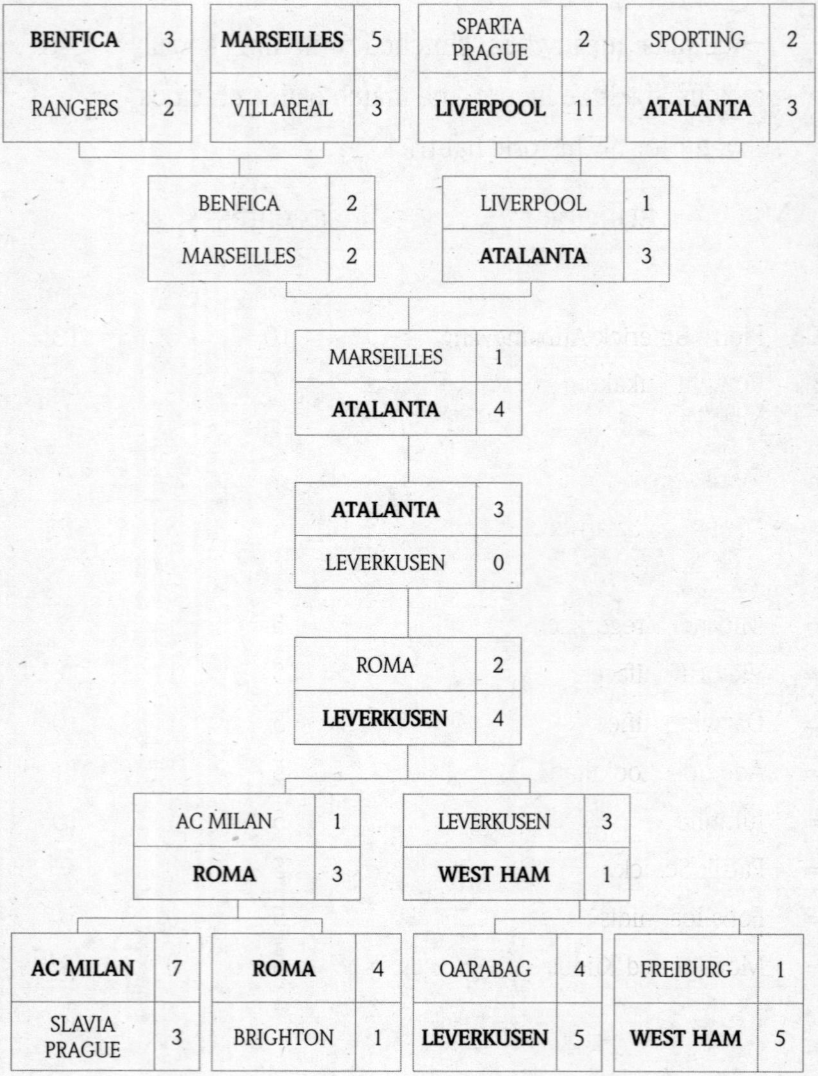
BENFICA 3
RANGERS 2
MARSEILLES 5
VILLAREAL 3
SPARTA PRAGUE 2
LIVERPOOL 11
SPORTING 2
ATALANTA 3
BENFICA 2
MARSEILLES 2
LIVERPOOL 1
ATALANTA 3
MARSEILLES 1
ATALANTA 4
ATALANTA 3
LEVERKUSEN 0
ROMA 2
LEVERKUSEN 4
AC MILAN 1
ROMA 3
LEVERKUSEN 3
WEST HAM 1
AC MILAN 7
SLAVIA PRAGUE 3
ROMA 4
BRIGHTON 1
QARABAG 4
LEVERKUSEN 5
FREIBURG 1
WEST HAM 5

EUROPA LEAGUE TOP SCORERS				
		Goals	Assists	Games
1	Pierre-Emerick Aubameyang	10	3	13
2	Romelu Lukaku	7	1	13
3=	Gianluca Scamacca	6	1	11
3=	João Pedro	6	0	6
5=	Mohamed Salah	5	3	9
5=	Viktor Gyökeres	5	2	9
5=	Michael Gregoritsch	5	1	8
5=	Victor Boniface	5	1	8
5=	Darwin Núñez	5	1	10
5=	Ademola Lookman	5	1	11
5=	Juninho	5	1	10
5=	Patrik Schick	5	0	9
5=	Fotis Ioannidis	5	0	6
5=	Mohammed Kudus	5	0	9

TOP 5 TEAMS

Free-flowing football. Devastating attacks. Dynamic defences. These five teams dominated their opponents, racking up victories and collecting trophies for fun.

1 BAYER LEVERKUSEN

Rival fans had a simple nickname for Bayer Leverkusen: Neverkusen. Why never? Well, they **never** won trophies! In fact, despite coming runners-up on five separate occasions, they'd never lifted the Bundesliga title. Their last trophy came in 1993 with the German Cup. But the 2023–24 season was to change all that!

From the first game until almost the very last, Bayer Leverkusen transformed into Bayer Never-lose-en. They just couldn't lose! Win followed win followed win. And after they beat Bayern Munich in February, their dreams of the title looked to be coming true. There were last-minute goals, unbelievable comebacks and dominant displays that ultimately ended Bayern Munich's incredible run of eleven league titles in a row.

Leverkusen set a new record for the longest unbeaten run (an incredible 51 games) and became the first team in the history of German football to win the double undefeated. If it wasn't for defeat in the Europa League final to Atlanta, it truly would have been the perfect season.

2 MANCHESTER CITY

No team in the history of English football had ever won four consecutive league titles. But that's exactly what Pep Guardiola's Manchester City side achieved when they got their hands on the Premier League title yet again! Even with star striker Erling Haaland sidelined for two months and with chief creator Kevin De Bruyne unavailable for the first half of the season, City did what they always seem to do: win. A thirty-five-game unbeaten run saw them claim the Premier League title on the final day of the season.

Fans were left wondering what might have been, however, as Pep's side were eliminated from the Champions League by Real Madrid on penalties (despite 'winning' both legs on xG – expected goals).

3 REAL MADRID

They always find a way to win, even when they're made to suffer by their opponents. Winners of the Champions League for a record-breaking fifteenth time. La Liga champions, having only lost one league game all season. Spanish Supercup champions. Three victories out of three against bitter rivals Barcelona.

Yet at the start of the 2023–24 season, things weren't looking so rosy. Questions were being asked of manager Carlo Ancelotti after Real had finished the previous season with losing the league title to Barcelona and had been hammered by Manchester City in the Champions League.

A tweak in formation, with Jude Bellingham at the top of a diamond midfield, transformed Madrid's season. Conceding just 26 goals in 38 league games they were mean in defence, and free in attack. Alongside Bellingham, Rodrygo and Vinícius Júnior ran wild, scoring eighty-seven league goals and coming up with big goals in big moments . . . especially in the Champions League!

Real Madrid are the most successful team in history. And with talents such as Kylian Mbappé and Endrick set to join them, it looks like there'll be no stopping them in 2024–25.

4 BARCELONA FEMENÍ

Five years ago Barcelona had never won the Champions League. Now, they've won it three times. And the Champions League wasn't the only title they won in 2023–24. A triumphant 25 wins in 26 games was more than enough to clinch the Liga F. They were also victorious in the Copa de la Reina and Spanish Supercup, giving them an incredible quadruple. In a team stacked full of World Cup winners and superstars, their possession-based football is a joy to watch. Their skill had never been in question, but there were doubts around their mentality and experience. Doubts which vanished once Barcelona finally – for the first time ever – beat Lyon. And they picked the perfect time to do it: in the Champions League final.

5 WREXHAM

In their first season back in the English Football League for sixteen years, Wrexham didn't just make up the numbers . . . they blew away their opponents!

With 88 points from 46 games, the Red Dragons secured second place and their second consecutive automatic promotion. Once again, star striker Paul Mullin was on fire. He scored 24 goals in 38 games (the best goal ratio in the league!), which was enough to win him the PFA League Two Fans' Player of the Year award.

Though Wrexham suffered seven defeats on the road (including a shocking 5–0 loss against Stockport

County), they made their Racecourse ground a fortress with 17 wins from 23 games. It was the best record in the league, the place that saw them record impressive victories over champions Stockport and Mansfield Town, as well as thumping 6–0 wins over Forest Green Rovers and Morecambe.

With Hollywood owners Ryan Reynolds and Rob McElhenney backing their squad and experienced manager Phil Parkinson calling the shots, Wrexham won't just be competing in League One – they'll be going for promotion once more!

EUROPA CONFERENCE LEAGUE

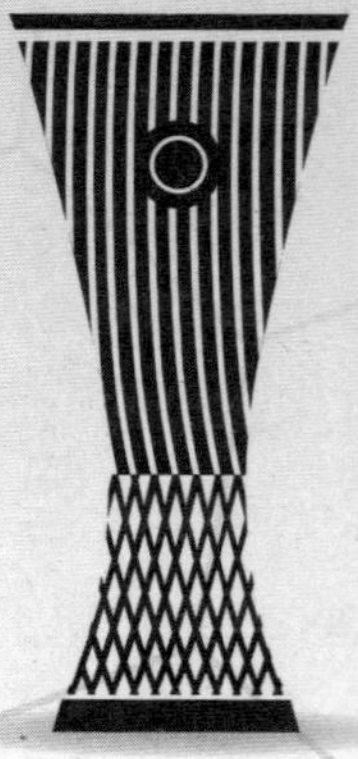

EUROPA CONFERENCE LEAGUE REVIEW

Wednesday 29 May 2024 was the date of destiny. Not just for Olympiakos Football Club, but for all of Greece.

This was the day when Olympiakos had the chance to make history. If they beat Italian side Fiorentina in the Europa Conference League final, they would become the first ever Greek team to win a European trophy.

What's more, they could do it in their own backyard – at the OPAP Arena in Athens, just a handful of kilometres from their home ground.

For Ayoub El Kaabi, the final offered an opportunity to add a fairytale ending to an extraordinary season. The thirty-year-old striker had played for clubs all around the globe – from his home country of Morocco to China, Turkey, Qatar and now, as of the 2023–24 season, Greece.

He may have been a journeyman, but Ayoub had settled in remarkably quickly to his new surroundings and gone on to score more than thirty goals in his debut season for Olympiakos.

'Olympiakos feels like home,' he explained to midfielder Santiago Hezze. 'I love it here.'

'And Olympiakos loves you . . . especially if you keep scoring goals,' Santiago replied.

Five of those thirty goals had come during the two-legged semi-final against Aston Villa, as Ayoub's one-man demolition job had blown away the high-flying English side. That result followed the pattern that Olympiakos had set throughout the knockout stages of the competition – delivering surprise after surprise on their way to becoming the first Greek team to reach a European final for more than fifty years.

There was the gutsy penalty shootout defeat of Fenerbahçe, in front of more than 40,000 screaming Turkish fans. A goal in each leg from Ayoub had seen off Hungarian champions Ferencváros. Most astonishing of all was the 6–1 thrashing of Maccabi Tel Aviv to overturn a 4–1 deficit from the first leg, helped in no small part by another three goals from Ayoub in the tie.

Now an even more formidable obstacle stood in their way.

'Fiorentina have got some serious European pedigree,' goalkeeper Konstantinos Tzolakis said to his teammates on the day of the final. 'This will be their sixth European final. They even reached the final of this competition last year.'

'They've got some seriously good players too, including loads of top internationals,' added Daniel Podence. 'Argentina winger Nicolás González, Brazil midfielder Arthur Melo, Italy star Giacomo Bonaventura . . .'

'We've been springing surprises all season. Who's to say we haven't got another shock up our sleeves?' replied Ayoub in confident mood.

'That's right, boys, and don't forget . . .' Everyone looked up as the dressing room door swung open. It was José Luis Mendilibar, Olympiakos' manager. '. . . I know a thing or two about winning European finals.'

Twelve months earlier, Jose had out-coached one of the greatest football minds on the planet – José

Mourinho – to lead Sevilla to Europa League glory against Roma. Their manager instantly filled the players with belief as the minutes ticked down to the biggest game of their lives. With José in charge, anything was possible.

A stadium packed full of their own fans helped too. The red-and-white stripes of Olympiakos dominated the violet of Fiorentina in the stands.

Such were the volume levels at kick-off that the noise from the supporters could have almost been heard in Italy. After three minutes, that noise seemed to grow even louder. Daniel surged down the left wing before cutting inside to draw a smart save from Fiorentina keeper Pietro Terracciano, who pushed his shot around the post.

A few minutes later, the Greek side were served a reminder of how dangerous their opponents could be. Following a clever corner routine, Nikola Milenković tapped the ball past Konstantinos, but the goal was ruled out for offside.

'Phew!' said Ayoub to Santiago. 'That was too close for comfort.'

From then on, chances were few and far between – but the best fell to Fiorentina. After pouncing upon a headed clearance, Giacomo Bonaventura could only side-foot his effort into Konstantinos' arms. Christian Kouamé had an even better opportunity in the second half when he found space in the penalty area, but his mis-hit effort was clawed away by Konstantinos.

'You're having a blinder!' shouted Ayoub.

'Hopefully there'll be some action at the other end soon,' the keeper replied with a grin.

But try as they might, Olympiakos couldn't make the breakthrough. With the game goalless after ninety minutes, the match entered extra time. If the tie was still all square after the additional thirty minutes, the final would be decided by a penalty shootout.

'I don't want a repeat of the Fenerbahçe match – my nerves can't take are more penalties!' Ayoub said to Daniel, only half-joking.

Yet as extra time drew on, a shootout appeared increasingly likely. After giving their all for nearly two hours in the Athens heat, both sides were tired and were struggling to create decent opportunities.

However, Ayoub and his teammates refused to settle for a draw. And with only four minutes remaining, they finally got their chance. Ayoub surged forward into the Fiorentina half. After finding André Horta in space on the wing, then making a run into the box, he narrowly failed to latch onto André's cross. The Italians frantically cleared the ball, only for Olympiakos to come straight back at them.

Now it was Santiago's turn to find space on the left wing. He whipped in a right-footed in-swinging cross.

The ball bounced once. Ayoub edged past his marker. He flung himself forward . . . and nodded it past Pietro Terracciano at the near post!

Cue scenes of utter joy and jubilation all around the stadium. Ayoub tore off his shirt as he charged away in celebration, his teammates close behind.

Olympiakos had done it . . . or had they? The referee hadn't confirmed the goal yet. The video assistant referee was checking if Ayoub had been offside. TV replays showed that it was a close call. *Really* close.

There was an agonising delay as everyone in the stadium waited and waited for the decision. Ayoub could barely watch. But finally, the verdict arrived.

ONSIDE! It was a goal! Olympiakos led 1–0! Cue more scenes of utter joy and jubilation

The star man had delivered again. The goal was Ayoub's eleventh in European competition for the season and set a record for the most goals scored in the European knockout stages, surpassing three giants of the game – Cristiano Ronaldo, Karim Benzema and Falcao.

But this was no time to think about individual records. Olympiakos were only minutes away from completing their own unique piece of history.

Fiorentina tried their hardest to muster a response, but time – and a wall of red-and-white stripes – were against them. There was no coming back.

When the final whistle sounded, the Olympiakos players sprinted to their fans; some collapsed to the ground, unable to believe what they had achieved.

Ayoub's goal had added Olympiakos to the prestigious list of clubs to have won a European trophy. He had also written his own unique place in the record books. Not bad for someone who had never even played in a European tie before this season!

AJAX	0
ASTON VILLA	4

STURM GRAZ	1
LOSC LILLE	4

OLYMPIAKOS	5
MACCABI TEL AVIV	5

UNION SG	1
FENERBAHÇE	3

ASTON VILLA	3
LOSC LILLE	3

OLYMPIAKOS	5
FENERBAHÇE	5

ASTON VILLA	2
OLYMPIAKOS	6

OLYMPIAKOS	1
FIORENTINA	0

FIORENTINA	4
CLUB BRUGGE	3

VIKTORIA PIZEN	0
FIORENTINA	2

CLUB BRUGGE	3
PAOK SALONIKA	0

SERVETTE FC	0
VIKTORIA PIZEN	0

MACCABI HAIFA	5
FIORENTINA	5

MOLDE FK	2
CLUB BRUGGE	4

DINAMO ZAGREB	3
PAOK SALONIKA	5

EUROPA CONFERENCE LEAGUE TOP SCORERS				
		Goals	Assists	Games
1	Ayoub El Kaabi	11	1	9
2	Eran Zahavi	8	1	8
3	Bruno Petković	7	0	7
4	Hans Vanaken	6	1	11
5=	Igor Thiago	5	1	10
5=	Fredrik Gulbrandsen	5	0	4
5=	Benjamin Nygren	5	0	5
5=	Gift Orban	5	0	5
5=	Dor Peretz	5	0	8
5=	Ollie Watkins	5	0	10
5=	Yusuf Yazıcı	5	0	10

TOP 5 GOALS

As referees added more minutes to stoppage time, games grew longer than ever before. Defenders became more tired, leading to more mistakes . . . and plenty more goals! From spectacular strikes to cool conversions, fans were treated to a range of incredible goals. Particularly these five . . .

1 ALEJANDRO GARNACHO (EVERTON 0–3 MANCHESTER UNITED, 26 NOVEMBER 2023)

Astonishing. Incredible. Jaw-dropping. Words don't exist to do justice to Garnacho's wondergoal. With just three minutes gone of this Premier League tie, Diogo Dalot hit a cross from the right wing. It appeared that the cross was overhit. It flew over the top of everyone in the penalty area and looked to be behind Garnacho.

Which is exactly when the young Argentinian winger scampered into action. He turned, ran six paces, and then launched himself into the air. With his back to goal, he connected with a bicycle kick from fifteen yards out. The ball flew from his right boot and soared into Jordan Pickford's top left corner.

Goodison Park was stunned. Garnacho crossed himself in gratitude, then jumped into Ronaldo's iconic 'siuuu' celebration. A fitting celebration for a wonderful goal.

2 JADEN PHILOGENE (ROTHERHAM 1–2 HULL CITY, 13 FEBRUARY 2024)

The Puskás award was created for moments like this. Having already scored one wondergoal earlier in the season (with a solo effort against Preston), Philogene went even better with this moment of magic.

Faking to shoot, Philogene dropped his right shoulder and nutmegged Rotherham's Oliver Rathbone. Rathbone turned and desperately chased back, only for Philogene to lure him in once more with a touch out of his feet, then send him for another hot dog with a sharp chop back. Rathbone was beaten, but Philogene was now facing backwards, six yards from the byline and almost at the edge of the penalty area. Worse still, there were four defenders AND a goalkeeper between him and the goal.

At such a tight angle, most attackers would have thought about passing to a teammate. Not Philogene.

Instead, he swung his right foot behind his standing left to produce an audacious rabona. The ball curled from his boot, lobbed Rotherham's keeper, and nestled in the net. His teammates went wild! The crowd went wild! And all around the world, viewers liked, shared and reposted.

3 LAUREN HEMP (MANCHESTER CITY 2–0 LEICESTER CITY, 4 FEBRUARY 2024)

Jess Park starts the move as she skips past two players before playing the ball inside to Hemp to beat a third. Hemp takes a touch out of her feet and then accelerates forward. Looking up, she spots 'Bunny'

Shaw who's peeled off to the right of the penalty area. She finds the attacker with a left-footed pass before continuing her run into the box. Shaw cuts back to beat the first defender, then delivers a cross into the middle of the area.

At first it seems Hemp has sprinted too far forward, but as the ball flies across the area she takes several steps back and then twists and turns her body into the path of the ball. Connecting with her left heel, the ball curves around Leicester keeper Lize Kop and into the net!

4 FEDERICO VALVERDE (REAL MADRID 3–3 MANCHESTER CITY, 9 APRIL 2024)

Valverde doesn't score normal goals. And this particular abnormal goal was of incredible importance, levelling a Champions League tie that Real Madrid would ultimately sneak through on penalties.

Veteran midfielder Luka Modrić drives forward and finds Vinícius Jr on the left-hand side of the area.

He looks up and plays a deep left-footed cross to the onrushing Valverde, whose sensational volley scorches the turf as it zooms past Stefan Ortega from just inside the penalty area.

5 MOHAMMED KUDUS (WEST HAM 5–0 FREIBURG, 14 MARCH 2024)

West Ham's summer signing from Ajax made quite the impression with some remarkable goals. There was the overhead kick against Manchester City on the last day of the 2023–24 season, but we've gone for his solo effort against Freiburg as the pick of the bunch.

Collecting the ball deep inside his own half, the Ghanaian attacker has one thing on his mind: attacking! He accelerates past one midfielder, then dribbles past a second. Now he's charging toward the defence, who are backing away. Freiburg's midfielders are chasing after him but none of them can catch him! Kudus is getting quicker and quicker. The ball seems to be glued to his right foot. With a desperate attempt, Freiburg's centre back steps forward to tackle, but Kudus skips past him as if he isn't there. As Kudus reaches the penalty area he looks up, aims, then fires past the keeper's left. The ball nestles in the goal, capping off a wonderful goal and a wonderful display from the Hammers!

SERIE A

SERIE A REVIEW

Lautaro Martínez beamed at his manager.

'It would be an absolute honour, boss,' he told Simone Inzaghi. 'I will wear the captain's armband with pride.'

'You are exactly what we need as our skipper – a great leader, strong and determined,' Simone replied. 'No wonder they call you *El Toro* ("The Bull").'

Lautaro couldn't contain his excitement. He had skippered the team occasionally in the past, but this was something entirely different. For the 2023–24 season, he would be the official captain of Inter Milan, one of the greatest clubs in Italian football.

'I will not let you down,' the Argentinian star said to himself, walking away from his meeting with Simone. Still smiling, of course.

The smile soon turned to a more serious look, though, when his thoughts turned to the season ahead.

Winning the league with the Nerazzurri had been a career highlight, but that had been back in 2021. Even though he had since lifted the 2022 World Cup with Argentina, Lautaro was still itching to repeat that success with Inter and lead them to another title.

But it would be a monumental challenge, particularly with the formidable AC Milan – Inter's long-time rival – standing in their way.

'Both Inter and AC have won nineteen league titles,' Lautaro explained to his new teammate Marcus Thuram, who had joined the club from Borussia Mönchengladbach. 'Whoever gets to twenty first will have ultimate bragging rights.'

'I promise AC will do everything they can to stop us,' added Turkish midfielder Hakan Çalhanoğlu. If anyone knew how deep the rivalry ran, it was Hakan – he had moved from AC Milan to Inter in 2021.

Over the summer of 2023, Inter had been strengthened not just by adding Marcus but also his France teammate, Benjamin Pavard, the Swiss stopper Yann Sommer and the permanent signing of wily defender Francesco Acerbi. It was time to find out how good the new squad could be.

'I want you to lead by example, Lautaro,' Simone told his captain on the eve of the season opener. 'Go out there and show your new teammates how it's done.'

Lautaro didn't need to be asked twice. Two goals against Monza, another against Cagliari and two more at home to Fiorentina – and three wins as well. It was a practically perfect start to the season, and the ideal warm-up for their big clash against AC Milan.

Playing their rivals at a packed-out San Siro stadium, it was Marcus who rose to the occasion. Tearing down the left wing, he terrorised the AC defence. In a breathtaking display of attacking football, the Nerazzurri plundered five goals, with Marcus's long-range thunderbolt the pick of the bunch.

If that result was extraordinary, what followed against Salernitana a fortnight later was even more remarkable. When Lautaro came on as a second-half substitute, the teams were locked at 0–0. By the end of the match, Inter had romped to a 4–0 win, with Lautaro bagging all four goals within twenty-seven crazy second-half minutes.

In the process, he became the first-ever player in Serie A history to score four goals as a substitute.

'Incredible effort today, skipper,' said Francesco.

'Maybe you should start as sub more often!' Marcus added with a wink.

Joking aside, Lautaro was loving starting alongside Marcus. The pair had quickly formed a lethal relationship up front and were causing opposition defenders no shortage of headaches. Rarely did a match go by in the run-up to Christmas when one of them wasn't on the scoresheet, and often both – as opponents Torino, Udinese and Lazio could testify.

Come the end of January, Inter led Serie A by two points. However, there was a familiar foe breathing down their necks: Juventus.

The giants of Italian football. In all, they had won thirty-six Serie A titles – and their eyes were firmly fixed on a thirty-seventh. On countless occasions in the past, Juve had ruined Inter's bid to be champions – and they were no doubt hoping to do so again when the teams met in early February.

'Forget what's happened in the past, boys. This is all

about today,' Lautaro encouraged his teammates before they ran out on to the San Siro pitch.

Chances were few and far between in an inevitably nervy encounter, with both sides desperate not to make a mistake. In the thirty-seventh minute, the visitors cracked, Federico Gatti chesting a cross into his own net to hand Inter the lead.

Juve threw everything they could at Inter as they battled for an equaliser, but there was no way past the rock-solid backline of Yann, Benjamin, Francesco and co.

When the final whistle sounded, the Inter players breathed a huge sigh of relief. Everyone was aware just how important this result could be.

'We need to press home our advantage and prove we should be champions,' Lautaro urged his teammates.

In each of their next four league games, Inter scored four goals, with only Roma managing anything in reply. Lautaro's brace against Lecce took his personal Serie A tally to 100.

Inter's positive run of results continued from winter into spring, and they extended their advantage at the top of Serie A. With Juventus's title challenge fading,

AC Milan led the chasing pack – yet such was the Nerazzurri's dominance that by the time they came face to face with their city rivals again in April, they were fourteen points clear.

This presented the tantalising option of Inter being able to win the Scudetto with victory over AC.

'This is our chance to become club legends,' Francesco explained in the dressing room. 'Never before in 116 years has either team won the league with victory in the Derby di Milano.'

'Let's make history, boys!' Lautaro roared.

With so much at stake, passions were running high on both sides. It was Francesco who struck the first blow, heading Inter into the lead after a flick-on from Benjamin in a slick set-piece move. The fact that Francesco grew up as a die-hard AC Milan fan must have made it all the more painful for the visitors.

Early in the second half, it got even worse for AC when Marcus set off on a superb solo run and smashed home another. It was party time for Inter and their fans. As the clock ticked ever closer to ninety minutes, all the noise was coming from the blue-and-black support in the San Siro.

Even a late AC consolation goal from England's Fikayo Tomori and a couple of heated squabbles in added time that led to three red cards couldn't dampen the mood.

'Peeeepppp!' When the final whistle, blew it was pandemonium. The San Siro exploded into cacophonous noise and smoke filled the air. Amid the jubilant scenes, Lautaro collapsed to the ground in disbelief.

Lautaro had led Inter to the Scudetto in his first season as captain, setting the perfect example for his teammates. He finished the season as Serie A's top scorer with 24 goals. His team had scored the most goals (89), conceded the least goals (22), and won the league by an enormous 19 points.

But there was one stat that mattered more than all the others. No longer were Inter and AC Milan tied on nineteen Serie A titles.

'Number twenty!' shouted Lautaro, lifting the famous Scudetto trophy high into the air. 'Bring on Number twenty-one!'

SERIE A FINAL TABLE							
Pos	Team Name	Played	Wins	Draws	Losses	Goal Diff.	Points
1	**Internazionale**	**38**	**29**	**7**	**2**	**67**	**94**
2	Milan	38	22	9	7	27	75
3	Juventus	38	19	14	5	23	71
4	Atalanta	38	21	6	11	30	69
5	Bologna	38	18	14	6	22	68
6	Roma	38	18	9	11	19	63
7	Lazio	38	18	7	13	10	61
8	Fiorentina	38	17	9	12	15	60
9	Torino	38	13	14	11	0	53
10	Napoli	38	13	14	11	7	53
11	Genoa	38	12	13	13	0	49
12	Monza	38	11	12	15	-12	45
13	Hellas Verona	38	9	11	18	-13	38
14	Lecce	38	8	14	16	-22	38
15	Udinese	38	6	19	13	-16	37
16	Cagliari	38	8	12	18	-26	36
17	Empoli	38	9	9	20	-25	36
18	*Frosinone*	*38*	*8*	*11*	*19*	*-25*	*35*
19	*Sassuolo*	*38*	*7*	*9*	*22*	*-32*	*30*
20	*Salernitana*	*38*	*2*	*11*	*25*	*-49*	*17*

SERIE A TOP SCORERS				
		Goals	Assists	Games
1	Lautaro Martínez	24	3	33
2	Dusan Vlahovic	16	4	33
3=	Olivier Giroud	15	8	35
3=	Victor Osimhen	15	3	25
5	Albert Gudmundsson	14	4	35
6=	Paulo Dybala	13	9	28
6=	Marcus Thuram	13	7	35
6=	Duván Zapata	13	4	37
6=	Hakan Çalhanoglu	13	3	32
6=	Romelu Lukaku	13	3	32

TOP 5 GAMES

End-to-end action! Mistakes! Nutmegs! Worldies! Red cards! Comebacks! Late winners! These five games had it all . . .

1 LIVERPOOL WOMEN 4–3 CHELSEA WOMEN (WSL, 1 MAY 2024)

Four days after being eliminated from the Champions League, Chelsea headed to Prenton Park knowing they simply had to win the first of their two games in hand. With Manchester City six points ahead – and with a nine-goal advantage – Emma Hayes' side not only had to win, they also had to rack up the goals. But Liverpool had other ideas . . .

Though Chelsea took a 1–0 lead, Liverpool came flying out of the changing rooms in the second half. They scored twice to make it 2–1, before Chelsea equalised in the eightieth minute. This topsy-turvy game was nowhere near done, however, as Liverpool regained the lead just one minute later. And two minutes after that, in the eighty-third minute, Chelsea equalised once more as Aggie Beever-Jones grabbed her second (and Chelsea's third) of the match. Fans were hardly able to stop and catch their breath!

Just as it looked like the game was heading for a draw, former Chelsea player Gemma Bonner stepped forward. The Liverpool centre back powered a header past Chelsea keeper Hannah Hampton in the ninety-second minute. Goal! 4–3. And there was still time for this crazy match to produce more action! Deep into stoppage time, Beever-Jones struck a clean volley which looked destined for the net . . . only for Liverpool keeper Teagan Micah to make an unbelievable save.

When the final whistle blew, the Chelsea players looked broken by the result. Manager Emma Hayes declared 'the title race is done'. After chasing a quadruple, it was looking like Chelsea were going to finish the season empty handed. Or was it?

2 COVENTRY CITY 3–3 MAN UNITED (FA CUP SEMI-FINAL, 21 APRIL 2024)

You could be forgiven for thinking this game was over after seventy minutes. With Manchester United cruising at 3–0 up, supporters were already planning their trips to Wembley for the final.

But this was 2023–24 Manchester United: a team that flicked between the sublime and the ridiculous (and at least five of their games could have made this list).

So when Coventry scored to make it 3–1, the Sky Blue fans started to believe.

Rather than treat the goal as a consolation, Manchester United started to panic. They lost their shape, their discipline, and their heads!

Eight minutes later, and feeling increasingly confident, Callum O'Hare's long-range shot took a wicked deflection and wrong-footed Andre Onana to make it 3–2!

Coventry continued to push forward – and deep into stoppage time, their moment came. Aaron Wan-Bissaka accidentally blocked a shot with his hand, leading referee Peter Bankes to award a penalty. Haji Wright dispatched the spot kick and the game headed into thirty minutes of extra time!

With both sets of players tiring, the game swung this way and that. Coventry went closest as Simms hit the crossbar! Then, in the final minute of extra time, the stadium erupted. Victor Torp bundled the ball home to complete a remarkable turnaround for Coventry. 4–3!

But wait! As the Sky Blues supporters celebrated wildly, VAR announced it was checking an offside.

Fans were made to wait . . . and wait . . . and wait . . . And eventually, by the finest of margins, the goal was ruled out.

The match would be decided by a penalty shootout. Casemiro missed Manchester United's first kick to give Coventry the advantage, but it was one they couldn't take. O'Hare and captain Ben Sheaf missed, while United scored their remaining penalties. The Red Devils breathed a collective sigh of relief. They'd done it. Just.

3 TOTTENHAM 1–4 CHELSEA (PREMIER LEAGUE, 6 NOVEMBER 2023)

Despite a fantastic start under new manager Ange Postecoglou, Tottenham's form began to suffer following injuries to key players. With plenty of discussion around 'Big Ange's' high defensive line, Spurs sought to get back on track against Chelsea, but the game was one of the most chaotic of the season. Five goals were scored. Five goals were disallowed (nice one, high defensive line!). There were nine VAR checks. Two red cards. And a ridiculous twenty-one minutes of stoppage time.

Dejan Kulusevski opened the scoring for Spurs after just six minutes. And then the trouble started. Destiny Udogie and Cristian Romero both survived VAR reviews for red cards, and Raheem Sterling and Moisés Caicedo both had goals ruled out for offside. Spurs may have been thinking it was their lucky night . . . until VAR picked up an aggressive challenge by Romero. After a review, Romero was shown a red card and Chelsea equalised from the penalty spot.

Half-time allowed everyone to have a breather, but not long after the restart, the chaos resumed when Udogie was shown a second yellow card and dismissed. Rather than sit back, Big Ange (who'd also been booked by this point) decided to keep his high defensive line and continue to press Chelsea high. It made for a fantastic watch . . . and it almost worked for nine-man Spurs!

Though Chelsea went 2–1 up through Nick Jackson, Spurs had chances to equalise. Eric Dier managed to get the ball into the net, only for his goal to be ruled out for offside. Then Rodrigo Bentancur went close. Ultimately, though, the nine men ran out of steam and Jackson scored two more late goals to complete his hat-trick.

4 ATLÉTICO MADRID 2–1 INTER MILAN (CHAMPS LEAGUE ROUND OF 16, 13 MARCH)

With a 1–0 lead from the first leg, Inter Milan doubled their advantage early on to make it 1–0 on the night and 2–0 on aggregate.

Game over? Not when your manager is Diego Simeone . . .

Just two minutes later, the ball deflected into the path of Atlético Madrid forward Antoine Griezmann. He spun and struck past Inter keeper Yann Sommer to give his side hope of a comeback.

Still needing a goal to take the tie to extra time, Atlético Madrid pushed forward. Yet Inter defended as if their lives depended on it . . . and as Atlético continued to throw players forward, it created more opportunities for Inter to counter-attack:

First Marcus Thuram had a one-on-one with keeper Jan Oblak . . .

Then Nicolò Barella had a one-on-one with Oblak . . .

But neither attacker could beat the Atlético keeper!

Atlético responded by throwing on substitute Memphis Depay, who quickly got to work. His strike finally beat Sommer . . . but cannoned back off the inside of the post!

Time ticked on. As the clock reached eighty-seven minutes, Atlético Madrid finally made the breakthrough – Depay angled a low shot into the corner of the net. The stadium erupted! And there was still time! While Inter hung on for extra time, Griezmann's low cross found Riquelme just yards from goal. He had to score! But the substitute blazed the ball over the bar. Atlético Madrid manager Simeone couldn't believe it! On the touchline he sank to his knees in disbelief.

There was only one way to decide this crazy game: with a penalty shootout! Oblak saved two penalties. Atlético Madrid scored three. After 210 pulsating minutes, it would be Simeone's men advancing to the next round.

5 CHELSEA 4–4 MANCHESTER CITY (PREMIER LEAGUE, 12 NOVEMBER 2023)

Manchester City sat seven points behind early season leaders Arsenal, while Chelsea were just three points below City. Both teams were desperate to win, which led to a game full of goals and entertainment.

Erling Haaland's early penalty put City 1–0 up, only for Chelsea's quick-fire double to swing the match in their advantage. City weren't done, though, and equalised just before half-time through Manuel Akanji.

Then in the second half, City turned the game once more as Haaland slid in to make it 3–2.

As the rain lashed down on Stamford Bridge, Chelsea pushed for an equaliser. Conor Gallagher's long-range shot was beaten back by Ederson . . . straight into the path of Nick Jackson! The Chelsea striker made no mistake to tie the game once more at 3–3.

By now it was anyone's game. Both teams pushed, but it was City who'd get the next goal! Rodri's deflected left-footed shot looped into the net, wrong-footing Chelsea keeper Robert Sanchez. City celebrated jubilantly, believing they'd won the game. But there was still time for one last twist.

Deep into stoppage time, Rúben Dias flew into a challenge with Armando Broja in the penalty area. He missed the ball, but connected with Broja. The referee was in no doubt: penalty!

Up stepped Cole Palmer. Signed months earlier from Manchester City, the Chelsea forward coolly dispatched the penalty, to bring this ridiculous match to an end.

BUNDESLIGA

BUNDESLIGA REVIEW

Florian Wirtz couldn't believe what he saw from the coach window.

Dressed in the red-and-black shirts of Bayer 04 Leverkusen, thousands upon thousands of excited fans lined the streets, shouting their support and encouragement. The sky had turned red and black too, from all the confetti being thrown in the air.

'I never knew so many people lived in Leverkusen,' Florian joked to his teammate Victor Boniface during the slow coach journey to their stadium, the BayArena. The fans had all come for one reason: to cheer their team to glory against Werder Bremen. A victory would seal the first league title in Leverkusen's 120-year history.

Things like this didn't normally happen to Leverkusen. Five times they had finished runners-up in Germany's top division, the Bundesliga. In one particularly painful season, when they lost the title to

Bayern Munich on goal difference, some newspapers called the team 'Never-kusen'.

The nickname stuck.

'You will *never* be German champions,' opposition fans would cruelly sing.

'It will be different today,' Florian vowed as he got off the coach.

Just as it had been different all season – and a huge part of that was thanks to Florian.

The Wirtz family is football mad. Florian's dad Hans-Joachim is a former professional player, while his older sister, Juliane, plays for Werder Bremen in the Women's Bundesliga. Meanwhile, after representing FC Köln's youth teams, Florian joined Köln's bitter rivals Leverkusen as a teenager in 2020.

Leverkusen fans don't usually like players from FC Köln, but they quickly changed their minds about Florian. Their new attacking midfielder made an instant impact with his skill, creativity and ability to boss the play. At 17 years and 15 days, he became the youngest ever player to represent Leverkusen and, not long after, the youngest player to score in the history of the Bundesliga.

In 2022, however, his flourishing career was disrupted by a serious knee injury – which meant he had to miss the World Cup – so by the time the 2023–24 season dawned, a fit and firing Florian, now wearing the famous Number 10 shirt, was ready to make up for lost time.

'We've got a really strong squad of players,' he told Juliane before the start of the season. 'I think we have a good chance of winning something.'

There was Victor, the Nigerian international and star striker.

Granit Xhaka, the no-nonsense Swiss midfielder bought from Arsenal in the summer.

Jonathan Tah, the rock of the Leverkusen defence.

Alex Grimaldo and Jeremie Frimpong, the two fleet-footed, flying wing-backs.

Lukas Hradecky, goalkeeper and inspirational captain.

'But what about Bayern Munich? They always win the league,' Juliane replied glumly, bringing Florian back to reality.

His sister was right. Munich had been crowned

champions in each of the past eleven seasons and seemed almost unbeatable.

What's more, their team looked even stronger this year as they had signed Tottenham superstar and England's record goalscorer, Harry Kane.

But Florian believed this time would be different – after all, they had their own secret weapon: manager Xabi Alonso. 'In Xabi we trust,' he said to Juliane. 'Champions League, league titles, the World Cup, the Euros – he won the lot as a player! And if anyone knows how to beat Bayern Munich, it's Xabi. He played at the club for three years.'

When Xabi became Bayer Leverkusen's manager in October 2022, they were one place off the bottom of the Bundesliga. By the end of the season, Leverkusen had climbed all the way to sixth and even reached the semi-final of the Europa League.

Hopes were high for the 2023–24 season and the team got off to the perfect start against Leipzig, with Florian netting the decisive third goal in a 3–2 win.

'Goooaaalll!' shouted Florian. 'What a way to start the season.'

It quickly got even better. Leverkusen won 10 of their next 11 games, scoring a whopping 34 goals in the process, with Florian pulling the creative strings in midfield. There was one game they didn't win, though – against Bayern Munich, of course.

'Here we go again,' Florian groaned when Harry Kane headed Munich into the lead after just seven minutes. Alex's exquisite free kick got Leverkusen back on level terms later in the first half, but when Leon Goretzka tapped in with only minutes remaining, it looked like the reigning champions would ruin Bayer's day yet again.

This time, though, Leverkusen refused to read the script. After Jonas Hofmann was bundled over in the box deep into stoppage time, Exequiel Palacios smashed home the penalty to earn a 2–2 draw.

'You won't beat us this year!' Florian yelled, celebrating the last-gasp equaliser.

By the end of the year, they were still unbeaten and still top of the table. But Florian was determined not to get too excited.

'No one is crowned champions at Christmas,' he said

to Victor with a fierce look of determination.

In the new year, things got a lot tougher. Opposition teams changed their tactics in an attempt to stop the Leverkusen goal machine that had already plundered forty-six goals.

However, the goals kept coming . . . just a bit later on in the games than before. A last-minute winner against FC Augsburg – by that man again, Exequiel – was followed a week later by a ninetieth-minute winner from Piero Hincapié against RB Leipzig.

'You see, it pays to be patient!' Florian laughed with Piero after the final whistle blew.

By early February, when Bayern Munich arrived in Leverkusen, the home team held a two-point lead over their title rivals and had the opportunity to go five points clear.

'This is our chance to change history,' Florian said to his teammates on their way out to a jam-packed BayArena. 'Let's get rid of the "Never-kusen" name once and for all.'

It didn't take long for Leverkusen to show their superiority, with Josip Stanišíc breaking the deadlock after eighteen minutes. The fact the Croatian defender was on loan from Munich must have been extra painful for the defending champions.

Alex doubled their lead after half-time before a last-minute strike from Jeremie sealed an emphatic 3–0 win. The defence, expertly marshalled by Jonathan and keeper Lukas, ensured that Harry Kane didn't even have a shot on target, let alone score a goal.

If there had been any lingering doubts before the Bayern game, the 3–0 demolition job blew them away. Now bursting with belief, Leverkusen won their next seven Bundesliga games, meaning victory against Werder Bremen would guarantee the league title.

Some 120 years of waiting came down to this. But if there were any nerves among the Leverkusen players before the match, on the pitch they were as confident as they had been all year.

Fittingly, many of the stars of the season got involved in the act. Victor opened the scoring from the penalty spot before Granit slammed home a second from twenty-five yards. Then it was Florian's turn to take centre stage.

His first goal was a humdinger from outside the box. When he broke clear from the halfway line to slot home a second, some fans were so overcome with excitement that they ran onto the pitch. After the supporters had finally returned to the stands, Florian drifted past the Werder defence – and through a haze of red smoke – to bury a right-footed strike into the far corner.

It was his first hat-trick in senior football but, far more importantly, it secured Bayer Leverkusen a 5–0 win and a first ever league title.

'*Championes, championes, olé, olé, olé!*' Florian sang with his teammates, while a sea of red-and-black-clad fans surged onto the pitch again at the final whistle. 'We are top of the league!'

The party continued long into the night – in the dressing room and all over Leverkusen.

After the celebrations finally died down, there were still five league games to go. Xabi refused to let his team relax, even though the title was in the bag,

'I want to make another piece of history,' Xabi told Florian and his teammates. 'Let's complete the season undefeated.'

Five games later – with yet another last-minute equaliser along the way – history was made.

Twenty-eight wins, six draws, zero defeats.

Eighty-nine goals scored and only 24 conceded.

The first ever team to complete a Bundesliga season undefeated.

A first trophy since winning the German Cup way back in 1993.

And that 'Never-kusen' name? Never again!

BUNDESLIGA FINAL TABLE							
Pos	Team Name	Played	Wins	Draws	Losses	Goal Diff.	Points
1	**Bayer 04 Leverkusen**	**34**	**28**	**6**	**0**	**65**	**90**
2	VfB Stuttgart	34	23	4	7	39	73
3	FC Bayern München	34	23	3	8	49	72
4	RB Leipzig	34	19	8	7	38	65
5	Borussia Dortmund	34	18	9	7	25	63
6	Eintracht Frankfurt	34	11	14	9	1	47
7	TSG 1899 Hoffenheim	34	13	7	14	0	46
8	1. FC Heidenheim	34	10	12	12	-5	42
9	SV Werder Bremen	34	11	9	14	-6	42
10	SC Freiburg	34	11	9	14	-13	42
11	FC Augsburg	34	10	9	15	-10	39
12	VfL Wolfsburg	34	10	7	17	-15	37
13	1. FSV Mainz 05	34	7	14	13	-12	35
14	Borussia Mönchengladbach	34	7	13	14	-11	34
15	1. FC Union Berlin	34	9	6	19	-25	33
16	*VfL Bochum*	*34*	*7*	*12*	*15*	*-32*	*33*
17	*1. FC Köln*	*34*	*5*	*12*	*17*	*-32*	*27*

BUNDESLIGA TOP SCORERS				
		Goals	Assists	Games
1	Harry Kane	36	8	32
2	Serhou Guirassy	28	2	28
3	Loïs Openda	24	7	34
4	Deniz Undav	18	9	30
5	Maximilian Beier	16	1	33
6=	Ermedin Demirovic	15	9	33
6-	Andrej Kramaric	15	6	30
8=	Victor Boniface	14	8	23
8-	Benjamin Sesko	14	2	31
10	Donyell Malen	13	1	27

TOP 5 SIGNINGS

In every transfer window, fans demand that their clubs spend loads of money to recruit their next superstars! While Financial Fair Play rules prevented many sides from going too big, there were still plenty of new signings made – and plenty of new heroes created. At £100 million, Declan Rice's move from West Ham to Arsenal was one of the priciest, with Jude Bellingham's £88 million to Real Madrid also costing a fair amount. While Bellingham was probably the best transfer of the season, we are going to feature him in the top 5 players category, so we're going to shine a light on five other excellent moves…

1 COLE PALMER (MANCHESTER CITY TO CHELSEA: £42.5 MILLION)

Is anyone else feeling a little . . . cold? Chelsea splashed the cash around this season, but their best buy was undoubtedly an unproven midfielder from Manchester City by the name of Cole Palmer.

Palmer had to be patient, waiting until October to make his first start in the Premier League for Chelsea (and just the fourth start in his career). But once in the team, there was absolutely no way he was leaving. Possessing ice-cold composure, unbelievable dribbling ability and a true eye for goal, 'Cold' Palmer powered Chelsea to European qualification. With an unbelievable 22 goals and 11 assists in 34 appearances, he became only the third player in Premier League history to be involved in more than 30 goal involvements aged 21 or younger.

Had Chelsea become Cole Palmer FC? Well, when illness prevented Palmer from lining up against Arsenal, Chelsea manager Mauricio Pochettino claimed it was a good challenge for Palmer's teammates. 'This is Chelsea Football Club, not Cole Palmer Football Club,' he said.

The result without Palmer? A 5–0 defeat . . .

2 GRIMALDO (BENFICA TO BAYER LEVERKUSEN: FREE)

For any attacking player, 12 goals and 17 assists in 51 appearances are fantastic numbers. But here's the plot twist . . . Grimaldo is actually a defender!

One of Xabi Alonso's rampaging wing backs, Grimaldo was vital in Leverkusen's invincible German season. He proved himself lethal from free kicks, and his wand of a left foot was not only magical from dead balls, but also when crossing from the wings. But of course, all defenders must be able to defend, and as part of a defence that conceded just 24 goals in 34 games, Grimaldo showed he was more than capable of keeping the ball out of the net.

Quick, energetic and tactically smart, Grimaldo's exceptional season in Leverkusen was rewarded with an international call-up for Spain.

3 HARRY KANE (TOTTENHAM TO BAYERN MUNICH: £100 MILLION)

Tottenham's all-time top scorer was not cheap. Bayern Munich knew they'd have to pay a premium to persuade the superstar to move to Germany. And as soon as he arrived in Munich, Kane proved just how much of a superstar he is.

It wasn't just the quantity of goals he scored – it was also the quality! One of his earliest was also one of his best. In a Bundesliga game against Darmstadt, Kane received the ball just inside his own half. Looking up, he saw the goalkeeper off his line . . . so he went for it! He may have been 56.4 metres from goal, but his shot soared over the keeper and then dipped under the bar just in time. A true wonder-goal!

The three goals and one assist that Kane bagged that day contributed toward his season total of 44 goals and 12 assists in just 45 games: a new record. With such stats, Kane lived up to the hype surrounding his transfer with one of the finest debut seasons in history. He scored goals at an even quicker rate in the Bundesliga than elite strikers Erling Haaland and Robert Lewandowski ever managed. Unfortunately, Kane's teammates didn't get the memo. Despite his brilliance, Bayern went trophy-less for the first time since 2012!

4 LIONEL MESSI (PSG TO INTER MIAMI: FREE),

In the 2023–24 season, we found out what would happen if the Ballon d'Or holder – and arguably the Greatest of all Time – moved to Major League Soccer. The answer? He'd transform his club on AND off the pitch, score goals for fun and continue to create jaw-dropping moments.

Subbed on for his debut in late July, Messi had a fairytale start to life in North America. Just minutes after entering the pitch, he won the game in stoppage time for his new team by scoring directly from a free kick. It was Miami's first win in 10 games! The madness continued as Messi's 11 goals and five assists in just 14 appearances lifted his team from last place in the MLS Eastern Conference to the US Open Cup final and the club's first ever trophy: the Leagues Cup.

5 DECLAN RICE (WEST HAM TO ARSENAL: £100 MILLION)

We all knew that Declan Rice was amazing at stopping goals with his tackling and interceptions from midfield. But what we didn't know was just how good he could be at scoring them!

When he signed for Arsenal from West Ham for £100 million at the start of the season, people questioned how Rice would adapt to playing for a team who liked to dominate possession. The answer? Easily!

Already one of the world's best defensive midfielders, Rice developed his game to also become a box-to-box-style Number 8. Arriving late in the opponent's penalty area, his seven goals and ten assists showed a new side to his game. One that Arteta – and Arsenal fans – liked very much.

LA LIGA

LA LIGA REVIEW

'Wowwwwww!'

Everywhere Jude Bellingham looked, there was another superstar:

Vinícius Junior, the Brazilian hotshot.

Thibaut Courtois, the keeper with the safest hands in the game.

Luka Modrić and his fellow midfield maestro, Toni Kroos, who between them boasted an astonishing ten Champions League winners' medals.

Defensive dynamos Dani Carvajal, Éder Militão and Antonio Rüdiger.

As Jude looked around the training ground on his first day at his new club, Real Madrid, he saw some of the greatest players in world football – the *Galácticos*, as they were called in Spain.

And now he was one of them, after joining Madrid from Borussia Dortmund for a massive transfer fee of

£88.5 million in the summer of 2023.

'Don't worry, Jude,' said Real's manager Carlo Ancelotti, welcoming him with a warm handshake. 'You'll fit in just fine.'

'Thanks boss. Can't wait to get involved and make an impact!' Jude replied before dashing off to meet his teammates.

As it happened, Jude didn't have to wait long at all. Just thirty-six minutes in fact.

As half-time neared in the La Liga season opener against Athletic Club, Jude conjured up the magic touch that, even at the young age of twenty, had made him one of the hottest football prospects on the planet, with a beautiful side-foot volley into the net.

The next week it got even better – the England ace bagged two goals in a 3–1 win at Almeria, then followed that by heading the only goal at Celta Vigo.

'I thought you were meant to be a midfielder,' Vini joked to his new teammate.

'I am,' Jude replied with a grin. 'Just one who likes scoring lots of goals!'

'Wait until next week's game. Then you might get

to see what it's like to score in front of our fans at the Bernabéu.'

Jude had dreamed of playing for Madrid at the Santiago Bernabéu, one of the biggest – and loudest – stadiums in the world. But with ninety minutes on the clock against Getafe, his home debut was in danger of turning into a nightmare. The teams were locked at 1–1 and the Real fans – who *always* expected their side to win – were far from happy.

'Keep going,' Jude urged his teammates. 'There's still time to win this.'

With seconds left to play, he got his chance. A shot from Nacho was spilt by the Getafe keeper. Jude was the quickest player on the pitch to react, slotting home the rebound to seal a dramatic win.

The players and the whole stadium went berserk. The Real fans had a new hero, and, for the first time, they got to see Jude's trademark celebration: he stood with both arms outstretched, soaking up the applause.

What a start to the season it had been. Four games, four wins and five goals.

By the end of October, Madrid were locked in a

three-way battle at the top of the league with Girona, the surprise frontrunners, and Barcelona, their bitter rivals and next opponents.

'Why do they call our game against Barcelona "*El Clasico*"?' Jude asked.

'Because it's always a classic!' Luka replied. 'There's only one thing you need to know as a Real Madrid player – you *have* to beat Barcelona. And this time we're even more desperate than normal. Barça were league champions last season; we want our title back.'

Jude knew how it felt to lose a league title. Before his move to Spain, Dortmund had agonisingly missed out on winning the league on the very last day of the Bundesliga season.

'I never want to have that feeling of disappointment again,' he explained to Vini as they arrived at Barça's Nou Camp stadium.

Barcelona exploded out of the blocks, scoring after six minutes, and came within inches of extending their lead, twice hitting the post. As the match approached the seventieth minute, Jude made them pay for their misses.

There didn't appear to be much danger when a

clearance fell to Jude thirty yards from the Barça goal. However, a couple of quick touches and . . . BANG.

'Goooaaalll!'

Jude rifled an absolute screamer into the top corner of the net, silencing the stunned home fans.

Real were level. Game on!

Then, in added time, it got even better. A cross from Dani on the right wing was flicked on by Luka, right into the path of the onrushing Jude.

'Goooaaalll! 2–1!'

The England star had done it again. He was quickly getting a reputation for scoring last-gasp goals. Now it was the turn of Barcelona's fans to sit and watch Jude's now-famous celebration.

As the season went on, that celebration became a very familiar sight. Wearing the Number 5 shirt made famous by French superstar Zinedine Zidane, Jude was quickly becoming a legend in his own right.

Goals against Cádiz, Villareal and Almeria (again) helped earn important wins, while two more against Girona put Real five points clear at the top.

Jude had plenty of help from his teammates too. Vini

and striker partner Rodrygo bagged four goals in a 5–1 thrashing of Valencia, Luka curled home the only goal of the game against Sevilla, and a last-minute header from Lucas Vázquez snatched the points at Alaves, despite playing the last 40 minutes with only 10 men.

'We might be the league's top scorers, but our defence is just as important,' Jude said to Dani and Antonio after they had kept yet another clean sheet.

In all, from November to March, they stopped the opposition from scoring in ten La Liga games. And this was with Andriy Lunin – who had started just nine games for Real before the season – deputising in goal for the injured Thibaut.

By the time Barcelona visited the Bernabéu in April, Real were eight points clear of their rivals. Just one more 'El Clasico' victory would all but guarantee the La Liga title – for a record thirty-sixth time!

Just as they had done at the Nou Camp, Barça took the lead after six minutes, but Vini equalised from the penalty spot soon after. A similar pattern unfolded in the second half with the visitors going in front again before Lucas levelled it up.

When the match entered stoppage time, Real might have been tempted to settle for a draw that would have maintained their lead at the top of the table. But Jude once again had other ideas.

Lucas found some space on the right wing against a tiring Barça defence. His cross made it all the way to the far post where Jude was waiting to smash the ball into the roof of the net with his left foot.

'All hail the king!' Vini shouted during the wild post-match celebrations.

'What do you mean?' Jude replied with a puzzled look.

'You are the new king, Jude. The king of *El Clasico*!'

The rest of the season felt like a victory parade. An easy win over Cádiz – another goal from Jude and yet another clean sheet – followed by Barcelona's loss to Girona meant the trophy was coming back to Madrid.

Real were the league's top scorers, boasted the measliest defence and lost just one game all season. And in Jude – the boy who moved from Birmingham to the Bernabéu, via Borussia Dortmund, and who finished the season with nineteen league goals – they had a new superstar Galáctico.

LA LIGA FINAL TABLE							
Pos	Team Name	Played	Wins	Draws	Losses	Goal Diff.	Points
1	**Real Madrid CF**	**38**	**29**	**8**	**1**	**61**	**95**
2	FC Barcelona	38	26	7	5	35	85
3	Girona FC	38	25	6	7	39	81
4	Atlético de Madrid	38	24	4	10	27	76
5	Athletic de Bilbao	38	19	11	8	24	68
6	Real Sociedad	38	16	12	10	12	60
7	Real Betis Balompié	38	14	15	9	3	57
8	Villarreal CF	38	14	11	13	0	53
9	Valencia CF	38	13	10	15	-5	49
10	Deportivo Alavés	38	12	10	16	-10	46
11	CA Osasuna	38	12	9	17	-11	45
12	Getafe CF	38	10	13	15	-12	43
13	RC Celta	38	10	11	17	-11	41
14	Sevilla FC	38	10	11	17	-6	41
15	RCD Mallorca	38	8	16	14	-11	40
16	UD Las Palmas	38	10	10	18	-14	40
17	Rayo Vallecano	38	8	14	16	-19	38
18	*Cádiz CF*	*38*	*6*	*15*	*17*	*-29*	*33*
19	*UD Almería*	*38*	*3*	*12*	*23*	*-32*	*21*
20	*Granada CF*	*38*	*4*	*9*	*25*	*-41*	*21*

LA LIGA TOP SCORERS				
		Goals	Assists	Games
1	Artem Dovbyk	24	8	36
2	Alexander Sørloth	23	6	34
3	Robert Lewandowski	19	8	35
3	Jude Bellingham	19	6	28
5	Ante Budimir	17	2	33
6=	Antoine Griezmann	16	6	33
6=	Youssef En-Nesyri	16	2	33
8=	Vinícius Júnior	15	5	26
8=	Álvaro Morata	15	3	32
8=	Borja Mayoral	15	1	27

TOP 5 MANAGERS

These managers called the shots, taking their teams to new heights. While some came up with new tactics to get the best out of their players, others transformed team spirit and gave their teams the confidence to succeed. In a season of immense achievements from clubs around the world, here are five managers who were at the very top of their game.

1 UNAI EMERY (ASTON VILLA)

In just eighteen months, Spanish manager Unai Emery transformed an Aston Villa team which had been sitting three points above the relegation zone into Champions League qualifiers!

How did he do it? Well, largely with the same squad that had been struggling. However, he introduced a few tactical tweaks, such as . . .

The high defensive line: this reduced the space that

opponents had to play in, which meant they had fewer passing options – and kept on being caught offside!

Quick counter-attacks: using the pace of speedy forwards such as Ollie Watkins to attack when opponents were disorganised.

A box midfield: to create lots of overloads (where there are more Villa players than opponents) which break defensive lines.

Though Villa's European journey ended in semi-final heartbreak in 2023–24, defeated by eventual champions Olympiakos, Emery will hope to go even better next season.

2 MATT BEARD (LIVERPOOL WOMEN)

With victories against Arsenal and Chelsea and a double over Manchester United, Beard's Liverpool team surpassed all expectations. Despite having far less spending power than the WSL's big hitters and a squad with fewer household names, his possession-based style worked its magic, and Liverpool finished in fourth place. In doing so, they became the first club to crack the top four ceiling of Arsenal, Chelsea, Manchester City and Manchester United that has existed since 2019–20.

3 KIERAN MCKENNA (IPSWICH TOWN)

It wasn't too long ago that Ipswich Town were struggling in League One. But then, in December 2021, Kieran McKenna arrived. His impact was instant. He coached his side to play free-flowing football, which lifted their fortunes. So much so that the following season, McKenna's team were promoted to the Championship with a club record of 98 points, scoring more than 100 goals!

Despite such success, McKenna wasn't given lots of money to sign loads of new players for the Championship. Instead, he'd simply have to improve the ones he had.

With a handful of value signings and loan deals,

McKenna led the sixteenth most expensive squad in the Championship to second place! No wonder on-loan attacker Omari Hutchinson called his manager a 'tactical genius'.

4 XABI ALONSO (BAYER LEVERKUSEN)

Given it was his first full season in Germany, Xabi Alonso didn't do too badly. Leverkusen's fifty-one unbeaten games (in a row), a domestic double and the introduction of an exciting style of football all proved Alonso to be one of the very best in the game. He didn't have a limitless amount of money to buy new players. Nor did he have the best players in the world. But what he did have was the motivation to coach every single player in his squad so that they became better. Most importantly, Alonso gave his team an incredible amount of mental strength, which allowed them to fight until the very end of every game. With eighteen goals scored after the ninetieth minute, Alonso transformed Leverkusen into a team who never knew they were beaten.

5 CARLO ANCELOTTI (REAL MADRID)

'The game belongs to the players,' Ancelotti said. These were words that he lived by, and he gave his Real Madrid team the freedom to play and the confidence to win – over and over again!

Winning a record-breaking fifth Champions League title of his career confirmed him as the most legendary manager the competition has ever seen. And another La Liga title and Spanish Supercup weren't to be sniffed at, either.

While Ancelotti had a team of superstars at his disposal, what he achieved had not come easily. His relaxed style meant he could keep his whole squad of individuals happy and on top form. But don't be fooled into thinking all he did was create good vibes! His tactical tweaks (particularly changing his formation to a 4-4-2 with a midfield diamond) got the best out of his players' talents, allowing them to play as a true team.

SETH BURKETT

LIGUE 1

LIGUE 1 REVIEW

It was the news that shocked a nation. As the 2023–24 season approached, it was announced that Kylian Mbappé was planning to leave Paris Saint-Germain.

Kylian was the face of football in France. The captain of the national side. The star of the World Cup-winning team in 2018 who came so close to leading them to glory again in 2022. A hero to all PSG fans, with a trophy cabinet full of Ligue 1 titles, player of the season awards and Golden Boots. Football in France without him would be very different.

'If this is going to be your last season for the club, then I'd like you to give us a special leaving present,' said new PSG manager Luiz Enrique. 'The club won the league in 2022 and 2023 – let's win a third title in a row.'

'Well, I've always liked hat-tricks!' Kylian grinned.

Luiz wasn't the only new face at PSG that summer.

There were loads of other new players too. Winger Marco Asensio joined from Real Madrid, while Gonçalo Ramos and Randal Kolo Muani added more firepower up front. Kylian's France teammates, defender Lucas Hernández and right winger Ousmane Dembélé, also made the move to Paris, from Bayern Munich and Barcelona respectively.

'We've already won the World Cup together,' Kylian said to Lucas and Ousmane. 'Do you fancy winning the Ligue 1 title too?'

There was another face in the squad that was even more familiar to Kylian – his younger brother Ethan. Still only sixteen, Ethan was hoping to make his first senior appearance for PSG this season.

With so many new players in the PSG squad, it would take time for the team to get to know each other and gel on the field. The season began with a goalless stalemate against Lorient, followed by another draw with Toulouse, a late penalty cancelling out Kylian's opener.

A first PSG goal for Marco, and two more from Kylian – including a rocket into the top corner – earned a first win against Lens to cheer up the fans at the Parc des Princes.

'Nice assist, Lucas.'

'Even nicer shot, Kylian!'

The topsy-turvy pattern continued. One week a sensational win at Lyon; the next week a loss at home to Nice. In such an unpredictable start to the season, the only thing you could count on was Kylian, who bagged a brace in both games.

In October, however, it clicked. From here on, PSG steamrolled every team that came in their path, winning eight league games on the bounce. They plundered twenty-four goals along the way, with eight of them coming from Kylian alone. If his eighty-ninth-minute winner at Brest was special, his performance against Reims was pure class. Three goals – right foot, left foot, right foot – plus some inspired keeping from Gianluigi Donnarumma at the other end secured a 3–0 win. The result put PSG on top of Ligue 1 for the first time in the season.

'I told you I liked hat-tricks, boss,' Kylian laughed with Luiz after the game.

By now, the new players were so settled at PSG that they felt like part of the furniture. Ousmane notched his first goal for the club in a 5–2 thrashing of Monaco, a match where Gonçalo and Randal also scored – along with Kylian, of course.

'I thought you might like some company on the scoresheet,' Ousmane joked with Kylian as they walked off the Parc des Princes.

In the last match before the winter break, Kylian celebrated his birthday in style with a second-half double against Metz, and PSG stretched their lead over Nice at the top of the table to five points.

But the highlight of his day came in the ninety-second minute when Ethan made his senior debut for the club.

'That was the best birthday present I could ever ask for, bro,' Kylian said to Ethan.

'IN-CRED-IBLE,' Ethan replied. 'Now I've had a taste of the first team, I can't wait for my next chance.'

But it was no easy task breaking into a PSG side that oozed world-class talent in practically every position – and they carried on in 2024 where they had left off in

2023, piling on win after win.

Just when they seemed unstoppable, though, a run of three draws in a row in early March was an important reality check. Familiar foes Monaco and Lille were closing the gap on the leaders, as were second-placed surprise package Brest.

'We haven't won the league yet, boys,' Luiz warned his players. 'It's time to get back to winning ways and show everyone who's number one.'

Clearly, Kylian listened to what his manager was saying. In their very next match, he netted yet another hat-trick in a game where PSG blew away Montpellier by an emphatic 6–2 scoreline.

With the season back on track, PSG were determined not to give their rivals any more chances. Gonçalo grabbed crucial goals against Marseille and Lyon before Ousmane got in on the act with a brace at Lorient. Not to be outdone, Kylian also netted twice that day, in the process becoming the first French player to score twenty-five league goals in one of Europe's big five leagues in four consecutive seasons.

'Incredible effort, Kylian,' Ousmane congratulated

his teammate afterwards.

'Thanks. As nice as the personal records are, though, all I'm thinking about is helping us win Ligue 1 right now.'

By the end of April, he could finally stop thinking about it. When second-placed Monaco lost to Lyon, PSG were champions of France. Kylian had bossed Ligue 1 again, winning another player of the season award and topping the scoring charts for a record-breaking sixth year in a row. It was the perfect way to sign off his time with PSG.

'All good things have to come to an end,' Kylian said to Ethan as the season was drawing to a close. 'I'll miss you and everyone at the club, and especially the fans, but it's time for a new challenge.'

His brother gave his brother a hug, then smiled. "I just feel sorry for whoever your new opponents will be!"

FRANCE FINAL TABLE							
Pos	Team Name	Played	Wins	Draws	Losses	Goal Diff.	Points
1	**Paris-Saint-Germain FC**	**34**	**22**	**10**	**2**	**48**	**76**
2	AS Monaco	34	20	7	7	26	67
3	Stade Brestois	34	17	10	7	19	61
4	Lille OSC	34	16	11	7	18	59
5	OGC Nice	34	15	10	9	11	55
6	Olympique Lyonnais	34	16	5	13	-6	53
7	RC Lens	34	14	9	11	8	51
8	Olympique de Marseille	34	13	11	10	11	50
9	Stade de Reims	34	13	8	13	-5	47
10	Stade Rennais FC	34	12	10	12	7	46
11	Toulouse FC	34	11	10	13	-4	43
12	Montpellier-Hérault SC	34	10	12	12	-5	41
13	RC Strasbourg Alsace	34	10	9	15	-12	39
14	FC Nantes	34	9	6	19	-25	33
15	Le Havre AC	34	7	11	16	-11	32
16	FC Metz	34	8	5	21	-23	29
17	*FC Lorient*	*34*	*7*	*8*	*19*	*-23*	*29*
18	*Clermont Foot Auvergne 63*	*34*	*5*	*10*	*19*	*-34*	*25*

FRANCE TOP SCORERS				
		Goals	Assists	Games
1	Kylian Mbappé	27	7	29
2=	Jonathan David	19	4	34
2=	Alexandre Lacazette	19	2	29
4	Pierre-Emerick Aubameyang	17	8	34
5	Wissam Ben Yedder	16	2	32
6	Thijs Dallinga	14	2	33
7	Georges Mikautadze	13	4	20
8=	Terem Moffi	11	2	30
8=	Gonçalo Ramos	11	1	29
10	Arnaud Kalimuendo	10	1	30

TOP 5 CRAZIEST MOMENTS

Wouldn't it be weird if football was . . . normal? From furry pitch invaders to cases of mistaken identity, these five moments had us scratching our heads and doing double takes.

1 CAN THE REAL EDGAR IÉ PLEASE STAND UP?

Edgar Ié rose through the Barcelona youth ranks and made one appearance for their first team. After that, his career reads like an upmarket travel magazine. He played for clubs in Spain, Portugal, France, Holland, Turkey . . . and then in January 2024 he pitched up at Romanian side Dinamo Bucureşti.

After Edgar Ié's first few days at the club, officials grew suspicious. This well-travelled new signing spoke no English at all (even though they had been promised he did). Still, they gave him his debut, and though Edgar Ié wasn't atrocious, he certainly wasn't as good as you'd expect a former Barcelona player to be.

Edgar Ié went on to play four further times for Dinamo. Then, suspicion turned to accusation. It emerged that Edgar Ié had a brother called Edelino. Both had trained in the Sporting youth academy, but Edelino's career hadn't reached the heights of his brother's. Instead, he'd spent most of his time kicking around in the Portuguese fourth tier and the Polish leagues.

Edelino, it emerged, wasn't *just* a brother. He was an identical twin!

Dinamo officials began to panic. Had their new signing sent his brother to play for them instead? To ease their nerves, they demanded that Edgar Ié show them his driving licence. Edgar refused . . .

With Dinamo already battling relegation, the club made a statement that they'd definitely signed the right Edgar Ié, his brother had absolutely never played for them, and the league should certainly not punish them with a points deduction.

The case continues . . .

2 PRE-SEASON CHAOS!

The hundreds of fans who turned up to Gateshead's pre-season friendly against Dunston probably didn't expect the match to live long in the memory. But when masked men drove a hearse AND a Subaru onto the pitch, they realised they weren't just in for an evening of gentle football entertainment. The two vehicles didn't just stop there. They spun round and round in the middle of the pitch while throwing hundreds of leaflets from the windows. Two of the men then left the hearse in the middle of the pitch, jumped into the Subaru and drove away into the night. Unsure of what to do with the stranded hearse, the referee abandoned the match. Eleven men were later arrested.

3 CAN WE HAVE OUR BALL BACK?

Gateshead wasn't the only place disrupted by pitch invaders. In the Mexican second division, a match between Alebrijes Oaxaca and Dorados had to be stopped when a dog charged onto the pitch and stole the ball! Three stewards gave chase . . . but none could catch the speedy mutt.

Fortunately, this story has a happy ending. When it emerged that the dog was a stray, home club Alebrijes (who won 4–0 before the pitch invasion) decided to take the boisterous hound into their care. And once they finally got the ball back, they managed to see out the game and collect all three points.

4 THE REFEREE'S A LUTON FAN!

It's fair to say that Evangelos Marinakis is far from your ordinary football club owner. The Greek businessman, who also owns Olympiakos in Greece and Rio Ave in Portugal, has had his fair share of controversies in the past. He's been known to intimidate referees and has even been charged (and then cleared) with bribery and match-fixing. So when his team Nottingham Forest were denied three penalties in their important league fixture against Everton, how do you think he reacted?

Not well!

Marinakis was furious. He demanded that the club put out a statement that made clear how cheated they'd been.

Thanks to Forest's media team, the eventual statement wasn't quite as angry as Marinakis wanted, but it still made headlines around the world. It accused the VAR referee Stuart Atwell of being a Luton fan (Forest were just one point and one place above Luton, who were in the relegation zone) and finished by saying the club would consider its options.

The statement was viewed more than 40 million times on social media! And when Sky Sports pundit Gary Neville questioned Forest's actions, the club announced that it would also launch legal action against Neville!

In the end, Forest stayed up – and Marinakis's season got even better when his other team, Olympiakos, won the UEFA Conference League!

5 FREEDOM FOR PAPA

Luis Diaz enjoys a close relationship with his parents. So, when they were kidnapped in Colombia by the National Liberation Army, he was devastated! Though his mother was released by the kidnappers after just a few hours, they kept hold of his father and demanded a ransom. The whole world was outraged!

That weekend, Liverpool dedicated their 3–0 victory to Luis Diaz, with goalscorer Diogo Jota holding up Diaz's Number 7 shirt.

Nine days after the kidnapping, Diaz returned to action as a late substitute. In a strong display, the winger scored Liverpool's equaliser in their 1–1 draw with Luton. As he celebrated, he revealed a shirt which had a simple message: *libertade para papa* ('freedom for papa').

Four days later, his father was released!

And later that week, his proud parents were watching from the stands as Luis Diaz put in a star performance, scoring both goals in Colombia's 2–1 victory over Brazil. There were plenty of tears – but this time they were of joy.

SCOTTISH PREMIER LEAGUE

SCOTTISH PREMIER LEAGUE REVIEW

It had all come down to this. On his 700th club appearance and his 150th game for Celtic, Joe Hart had the chance to sign off his career in unforgettable fashion.

He had kept goal for England at the World Cup and Euros, played in cup finals at Wembley and Hampden Park, and won league titles in Scotland and England, including the most dramatic of them all for Manchester City (who could ever forget '*Aguerooooo!*'?).

But he had never experienced anything like this. Matches between Celtic and Rangers were always massive. The two biggest teams in Scottish football – one in green and white, one in blue, both from Glasgow – didn't just have the greatest rivalry in Scotland, but one of the fiercest in world football.

And this particular "Old Firm" derby was extra special. After thirty-six games of the season, just three points separated the two sides at the top of the league table. Victory for Celtic would mean the Scottish Premiership was almost theirs, but a defeat would hand the advantage to their rivals.

For Joe, a win would be the crowning moment from a hugely successful three seasons with Celtic. The keeper had enjoyed instant success in his first season when he won the League and League Cup, and it got even better in 2023 when the Hoops also bagged the Scottish Cup as part of a domestic treble.

Could Joe add another medal to his glittering list of honours?

Whatever the result, it would likely be Joe's last chance to become a league champion again. Back in February, he had shocked his teammates when he announced he would hang up his gloves at the end of the season.

'You can't retire, Joe. You've got the safest hands in Scotland,' said captain Callum McGregor.

'That's very kind, skipper, but I've made up my

mind,' Joe replied. 'I want to stop when I'm still at the top of my game, rather than someone else making the decision for me.'

'Well, we're going to do everything we can to make sure you go out on top.'

Back in the autumn, a nerve-jangling end to the season had seemed about as likely as Celtic and Rangers fans sitting down for a friendly matchday meal together. In their first derby, Kyogo Furuhashi's ferocious half-volley at Rangers' Ibrox Stadium stunned the home fans into silence. Danilo had two big chances to equalise in the closing minutes but was thwarted by Joe's heroics in goal.

A few weeks later, Joe went from hero to villain when he was sent off against Livingston after clattering into Mo Sangare outside the penalty area. Being down to ten men didn't seem to bother Celtic too much, though, as they cruised to a 3–0 win.

Joe was gutted. It was the first red card of his career.

'Thanks Matt. You and the boys saved my skin out there,' he said to his teammate Matt O'Riley in the dressing room.

'Makes a change from you saving us, Joe!' Matt laughed.

In November, Celtic hit Aberdeen for six, with South Korean sensation Oh Hyeon-gu netting twice in stoppage time, to stretch their lead over Rangers to eight points. Even a first loss of the season to Kilmarnock couldn't dampen the Christmas spirit and, at the end of December, the Hoops regained control with another win over Rangers. A volley from Paulo Gonçalves Bernardo was followed by another stunner from Kyogo for a 2–1 victory.

'The perfect way to get our New Year's Eve party started!' Kyogo shouted after the match.

But the Celtic manager Brendan Rodgers wasn't getting carried away: 'Let's enjoy our win, boys, but remember there is still a long way to go – and Rangers will be out for revenge.'

From his twenty years' experience as a professional footballer, Joe knew his boss was right.

'You can't take anything for granted in this game,' Joe told Kyogo, although even he didn't expect Rangers to put up *quite* such a ferocious challenge during the weeks that followed.

Celtic won their two league games in January, but Rangers won three. In February, the Hoops drew with Aberdeen and then, after they failed to beat Kilmarnock, the unthinkable happened: Rangers were on top!

There followed a thrilling tit-for-tat battle for the league title. Each time Celtic won, Rangers would do the same. And every Rangers victory seemed to be followed by one for the Hoops. Even when Rangers lost to Motherwell, Celtic suffered the same fate against Hearts twenty-four hours later.

The goals were flying in too. After Rangers thrashed Hearts 5–0, Celtic put seven past Dundee – with seven different players on the scoresheet.

'You were practically the only player who didn't score for us, Joe,' laughed Matt, Celtic's leading scorer.

'I prefer to focus on what's going on at the other end of the pitch,' Joe grinned.

The two teams were inseparable – and so when they went head-to-head again in March, a draw seemed inevitable. From the moment Daizen Maeda put

Celtic in front after just twenty-one seconds, the fans were treated to ninety minutes of explosive action, climaxing in a thrilling finale when Rabbi Matondo's wonder strike snatched a 3–3 draw for Rangers.

Joe threw his gloves to the floor in frustration in the dressing room. He never liked conceding three goals, particularly one in the final minute.

'We've let them off the hook once,' he growled at his centre-back duo Liam Scales and Cameron Carter-Vickers. 'We won't do it again.'

Playing with fire in their bellies, the reigning champions went on a blistering run of form. They would not give up their title without an almighty fight. Everyone played their part.

St Mirren were dispatched with ease. James Forrest marked his first start in five months with both goals against Dundee. While Kyogo and Matt did the damage up front against Hearts, Joe was in inspired form at the other end, pulling off big save after big save to keep a clean sheet.

It was an onslaught – and Rangers couldn't keep up. By the time the two teams met for their fourth and final league match of the season, Rangers faced the monumental task of having to win in front of 60,000 roaring Hoops fans at Celtic Park.

'Great to have you back from injury, skipper,' Joe said to Callum. 'We need to be at our very best today.'

The derby was settled by twelve mad minutes at the end of the first half. Matt continued his hot run of form to open the scoring, before an own goal from John Lundstram doubled the lead.

'We'll take whatever help we can get, boys – doesn't matter who scores for us,' Joe shouted to his teammates. "Stay switched on!'

But the Celtic players couldn't take their keeper's advice, and within two minutes, Rangers had halved the lead. Yet just when the away side thought they were back in the contest, a red card for a bad tackle meant they would have to play the rest of the match with only ten men. It proved a step too far – Rangers were powerless to stop Celtic from holding out for a third derby win of the season.

Four days later, a 5–0 thumping of Kilmarnock – their bogey team earlier in the season – sealed the inevitable:

Celtic were League champions again!

All that was left was for the Hoops to collect the trophy at the end of their final match against St Mirren at Celtic Park.

Normally, the captain lifts the trophy, but Callum had other ideas. After all, this was no normal day.

'Come on, Joe,' Callum said, beckoning the keeper forward to join him. 'Let's do this together.'

'Are you sure, skipper?'

'Of course. Besides, it's too heavy to lift on my own!'

JOHN MURRAY

SPL FINAL TABLE							
Pos	Team Name	Played	Wins	Draws	Losses	Goal Diff.	Points
1	**Celtic**	**38**	**29**	**6**	**3**	**65**	**93**
2	Rangers	38	27	4	7	55	85
3	Heart of Midlothian	38	20	8	10	12	68
4	Kilmarnock	38	14	14	10	2	56
5	St Mirren	38	13	8	17	-6	47
6	Dundee	38	10	12	16	-19	42
7	Aberdeen	38	12	12	14	-4	48
8	Hibernian	38	11	13	14	-7	46
9	Motherwell	38	10	13	15	-3	43
10	St Johnstone	38	8	11	19	-25	35
11	Ross County	38	8	11	19	-29	35
12	*Livingston*	*38*	*5*	*10*	*23*	*-41*	*25*

SPL TOP SCORERS				
		Goals	Assists	Games
1	Lawrence Shankland	24	4	37
2	Matt O'Riley	18	13	37
3	James Tavernier	17	10	38
4=	Cyriel Dessers	16	4	35
4=	Bojan Miovski	16	2	38
6	Theo Bair	15	6	38
7=	Kyogo Furuhashi	14	5	38
7=	Simon Murray	14	4	37
9	Abdallah Sima	11	2	25
10=	Luke McCowan	10	5	37

TOP 5 INCREDIBLE MOMENTS

Football is a game of highs, lows, and unbelievable moments. Fans gasp, commentators scream, and clips go viral as minnows overcome giants, records are broken, and new legends are made. If Hollywood scriptwriters were working on the 2023–24 season, these are five of the best stories they might have come up with . . .

1 THE CHAMPIONS LEAGUE HERO MADE IN STOKE

The Champions League semi-final between Real Madrid and Bayern Munich split the loyalties of Stoke City fans when two of their former misfiring strikers faced off against each other. Neither Real's Joselu nor Bayern's Eric Choupo-Moting had looked like world-beaters for the Potters. With just four goals in 34 appearances for Stoke (and six in 68 for Newcastle), Joselu wasn't exactly considered a magical goalscorer. And while Choupo-Moting fared a little better (five goals in 32 appearances), few fans could have predicted that the pair would end up playing for two of the best teams in the world.

Yet that's exactly what happened, and with Real Madrid losing 1–0 on the night and 3–2 on aggregate, manager Carlo Ancelotti turned to substitute Joselu in the eighty-first minute.

Just two years previously, Joselu had gone to the Champions League final as a supporter of Real Madrid.

Now, it was down to him to make sure they reached the final again.

Talk about rags to riches!

Just seven minutes later, something incredible happened: he scored! With eighty-eight minutes gone, Joselu pounced on a mistake by Manuel Neuer to equalise the match.

And Joselu wasn't done there! In the ninety-first minute, the Spanish striker swept home from six yards out to win the tie for Real Madrid!

Cue crazy celebrations, with everyone rushing to Joselu. The man considered not good enough for Stoke City was Real Madrid's unlikely hero!

2 A DRAMATIC UNBEATEN RECORD

With eighty-one minutes gone of Leverkusen's Europa League semi-final against Roma, it appeared their unbeaten record was about to come to an end. Losing 2–0 (and drawing 2–2 on aggregate), they were even facing possible elimination from the tournament!

But then their luck turned. A disastrous own goal from Gianluca Mancini gave Leverkusen the goal they needed to qualify for the next round. Yet they were still on track to lose their unbeaten record!

Rather than sit back and see out the tie, Leverkusen pushed forward to keep their unbeaten record. Then with the very last kick of the game, they got their reward! Josip Stanišić cut inside in the ninety-seventh minute and fired a low shot past Mile Svilar in the

Roma goal, to spark wild celebrations.

They'd done it! Another game unbeaten and a new record: Leverkusen had now gone forty-nine games unbeaten, more than any other European team had managed in history. They'd done so in the most dramatic way possible.

3 SAN MARINO CAN'T STOP SCORING

With a population of just over 33,000, the tiny European nation of San Marino aren't considered big-hitters in international football. They've never made a World Cup . . . or a European Championship . . . or even won a competitive game of football!

They're ranked at the very bottom of FIFA's world rankings for good reason.

But in qualification for Euro 2024, something incredible happened . . . they scored! It had been more than two years since their last goal. Alessandro Golinucci's equaliser against Denmark sparked wild celebrations. Though they couldn't hold on for the draw, a narrow 2–1 defeat allowed them to hold their heads high.

Furthermore, in the next game (a 3–1 defeat to Kazakhstan) . . . they scored again! It was the first time in eighteen years that they'd bagged a goal in back-to-back games.

Surely they couldn't score for a third game in a row?

But against Finland they went and did just that. Filippo Berardi's ninety-seventh-minute penalty was the first time in history that San Marino had scored in three consecutive games!

4 NEWCASTLE ANNOUNCE THEMSELVES IN EUROPE

For the first time in twenty years, Newcastle were back in the Champions League. Yet from the moment the draw was made, the task ahead looked tricky. Group F would be made up of . . .

AC Milan . . .

Borussia Dortmund . . .

PSG . . .

. . . and Newcastle United!

It was like a Who's Who of legendary European football teams!

Newcastle's opening game was a cagey 0–0 draw away to Milan. But it was the first home game that would prove truly special. St James' Park was packed. Fans belted out songs as Newcastle took on PSG, creating four walls of Toon Army noise. Such an electric atmosphere seemed to power Newcastle's players as they tore into their opponents.

PSG couldn't match Newcastle's energy or intensity as the Magpies raced into a 3–0 lead! To make it even better for the disbelieving fans, local lads Sean Longstaff and Dan Burn both scored! And not even superstar Kylian Mbappé could sour their night – the elite goalscorer managed just one shot on target and Newcastle recorded an historic 4–1 victory! Worth the wait? Newcastle's fans certainly thought so . . .

5 CUPSETS APLENTY!

David versus Goliath. Rags against riches. Haves versus have-nots. Cup competitions give small teams the opportunity to create BIG upsets – and this season we were really treated.

In England, semi-professional side Maidstone United caused one of the biggest shocks of all time by beating Premier League-bound Ipswich Town 2-1 in the FA Cup fourth round. Though Ipswich had 78 per cent of the possession and hit the post three times, they just couldn't beat the team ninety-eight places below them in the league pyramid!

In Germany, third tier Saarbrücken wrote their name into history. Their second-round match in the DFB-Pokal cup created international headlines when they beat German giants Bayern Munich with a ninety-sixth-minute winner! And they weren't done there. In the third round they overcame Bundesliga side Eintracht Frankfurt 2–0, then in the quarter-final they beat the Bundesliga's Borussia Mönchengladbach 2–1 to reach the semi-final!

EURO 2024

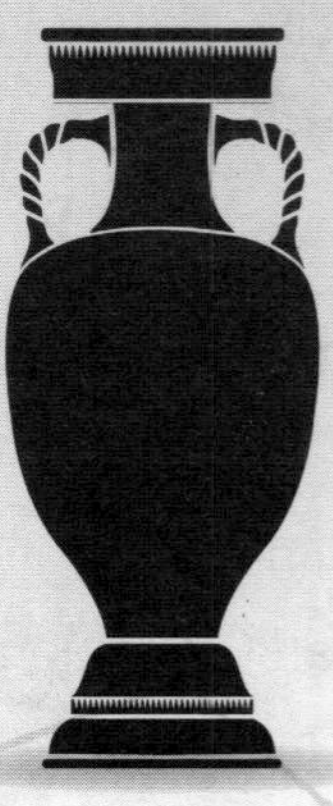

EURO 2024

". . . happy birthday dear Lamine
Happy birthday to you!"

It was the day before the Euro 2024 final and the Spanish players were eating cake.

A football cake, to be precise.

This wasn't the normal preparation for one of the biggest games of their lives, but then this wasn't a normal occasion. It was Lamine Yamal's birthday – and given how the young winger had lit up the tournament over the past month, it was definitely worth celebrating.

Exactly four weeks earlier Lamine had made history when he became the youngest ever footballer to play in the European Championships – at just 16 years and 338 days. He marked the occasion with an eye-catching performance in Spain's 3–0 win over Croatia, full of mazy dribbles, tricks and jinks, and capped by a beautifully weighted cross for Dani Carvajal to score. Everyone who followed Barcelona, Lamine's club team, already knew about the teenager's stunning talent; now the rest of Europe did too.

As the tournament progressed, Lamine's reputation as world football's next superstar grew and grew. There were impressive displays in wins over Italy and Albania, then a blistering performance in a 4-1 rout of Georgia, which included another assist – this time on to Fabian Ruiz's head.

In the quarter-finals, Lamine turned provider once again when he set up Dani Olmo's opener against Germany as Spain shattered the tournament host's dreams, but he saved his best moment for the semi-final win over France. Picking up the ball in the French half, Lamine turned left, then right, then left once more before curling a left-footed beauty into the top corner.

What a way to become the youngest ever scorer at the Euros! No wonder the Spain players wanted to give Lamine a cake.

"Thanks everyone. Let's hope we can have an even

bigger celebration tomorrow night," Lamine said to his team-mates after blowing out the candles.

"Don't get too excited, birthday boy – you're an old man now," joked team-mate Jesús Navas, who at 38 was the oldest player in Spain's squad.

"I know," Lamine replied with a smirk. "I'm nearly half your age!"

After six games, six wins and 13 goals, Spain stood 90 minutes away from greatness, the chance to win the country's fourth European Championship tantalisingly within reach.

"Tomorrow we have the chance to make history, boys. No team has ever won all seven of their matches at the Euros," coach Luis de la Fuente said to his players. "But it won't be easy. . ."

Standing in their way at Berlin's Olympiastadion on the 14th of July would be England.

After topping their group with one win and two draws, England were 90 seconds away from exiting the tournament in the last 16 when Jude Bellingham had conjured a spectacular overhead kick to equalise against Slovakia. Harry Kane then completed the turnaround in extra time.

It was a similar story in the next two rounds. Bukayo Saka hit a late equaliser against Switzerland before Trent Alexander-Arnold smashed in the winning penalty in the shootout, while Ollie Watkins was the hero of the semi-final, scoring a spectacular last-minute winner to sink the Netherlands.

"This England team doesn't know how to lose," Lamine said to Rodri, the midfielder who had played a pivotal part in Spain's run to the final.

"Nor do *La Roja*, my friend," Rodri replied, smiling. "We will never give up."

A mixture of sun and showers greeted the Spanish players when they arrived at the Olympiastadion on the day of the final. Once they stepped inside the ground, they were met by waves and waves of white shirts, with thousands of noisy England fans far outnumbering the red of their Spanish counterparts.

"Let's make sure we silence those fans tonight," Lamine said to Nico Williams, who had been another star of the tournament.

However, neither set of fans had much to cheer

about in a nervy first half. Nico caused panic among the English defence with some surging runs but – despite dominating possession – Spain couldn't create any clear chances. At the other end, keeper Unai Simon had to be alert to stop an effort from Phil Foden on the stroke of half-time.

Lamine, for his part, was struggling to make his usual impact after being well marked by England left-back Luke Shaw.

"Keep trying, Lamine," Nico said to his fellow winger as they walked off the pitch at half-time. "We know the chances will come in the end."

As it happened, Spain didn't have to wait that long. Two minutes into the second half, Lamine finally found some space on the right wing after escaping the attention of a couple of defenders. As he advanced towards the penalty area, he spotted Nico in space on the opposite wing and rolled the ball into his path.

Nico did the rest, his first-time shot leaving England goalkeeper Jordan Pickford helpless.

1–0! The deadlock was broken.

Lamine and Nico couldn't contain their joy, sharing a

massive hug of celebration.

"Great pass!"

"Great goal!"

Full of confidence, Spain set out to finish the job. Minutes later, Dani Olmo shot just wide, then – after another delicious through-ball from Lamine – captain Alvaro Morata's effort was cleared off the line.

The chances kept coming. Nico's rasping drive went the wrong side of the post. Then it was Lamine's turn to have a go. Cutting in from his favourite right wing, his left-foot strike seemed destined to find the corner of the net, but Pickford stuck out a hand to pull off a miraculous save.

England were hanging on but, try as they might, the Spaniards could not find the crucial second goal. On 73 minutes, their opponents made them pay for their misses. A slick exchange of passes – from Bukayo Saka to Jude Bellingham to Cole Palmer – set up a shooting chance for the Chelsea player, who drilled the ball home from the edge of the area.

All of a sudden, England were back level!

Despite the setback, the Spanish players refused to

let their heads drop.

"We almost won the game once," Lamine said to Nico and Dani Olmo. "Let's go out there and win it again."

The three players soon combined to cut open the English defence again. Nico powered his way to the edge of the area where he played the ball to Dani Olmo, who promptly flicked it back to his team-mate. Nico then passed to Lamine who had escaped his marker inside the penalty area, only for his shot to be blocked by a diving Pickford.

"What do we have to do to score?" Lamine wondered to himself, scarcely able to believe the heroics of the England keeper.

His team-mates soon provided the answer. Another sweeping move saw Dani Olmo link up with Mikel Oyarzabal, who in turn spread the ball wide to Marc Cucurella on the wing. His cross could not have been better placed, teeing up Mikel – who had continued his run into the penalty area – to prod the ball past the onrushing Pickford.

Spain had retaken the lead!

The Spanish players, everyone on the bench, and all

their fans around the stadium went berserk. The Euro 2024 trophy was almost theirs.

That would be Lamine's last involvement in the match, though, as he was substituted for Mikel Merino shortly after the goal. He never liked coming off the pitch but always respected the decision of his manager.

"Best of luck, Mikel," Lamine said to his team-mate. "I know you can help close this game out."

Even though there were only four minutes remaining, there was still time for not one but two England headers to be cleared off the line – the first thanks to Unai's hands, the second thanks to Dani Olmo's head.

There would be no further chances. As the match entered its 94th minute, the referee's whistle signalled the end of the final game of Euro 2024.

Players from both teams collapsed to the ground – a mixture of joy and despair – as everyone from the Spain squad charged onto the pitch to begin some wild celebrations.

After 51 matches, the tournament that had begun with 24 teams had ended with one very worthy winner.

Spain were European champions!

It was time for Lamine's second big party in as many days. As well as the Henri Delaunay Cup and winners' medals that the Spanish players paraded around the Olympiastadion, some individual awards were handed out too.

Player of the final? Nico.

Player of the tournament? Rodri.

Young player of the tournament? No prizes for guessing that one. The young player award was of course won by the youngest ever player in the tournament's history.

A player who we are going to be seeing plenty more of at many more European Championships in the years to come.

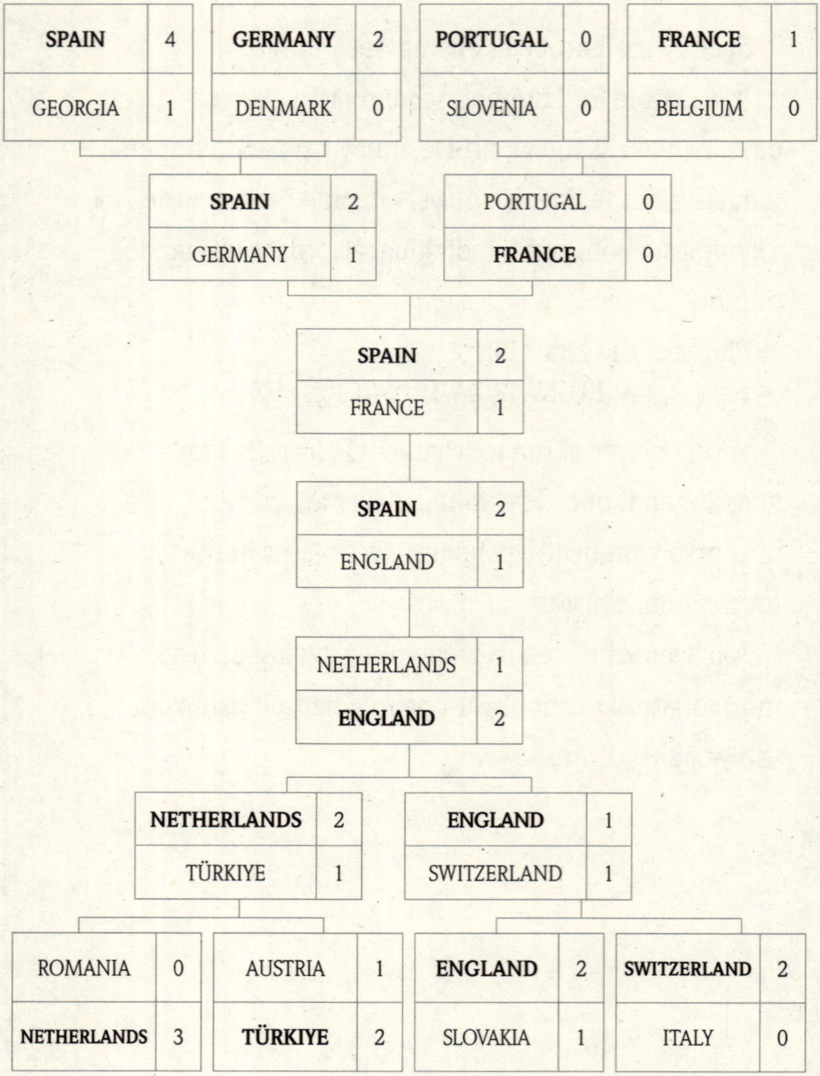
SPAIN 4
GEORGIA 1
GERMANY 2
DENMARK 0
PORTUGAL 0
SLOVENIA 0
FRANCE 1
BELGIUM 0
SPAIN 2
GERMANY 1
PORTUGAL 0
FRANCE 0
SPAIN 2
FRANCE 1
SPAIN 2
ENGLAND 1
NETHERLANDS 1
ENGLAND 2
NETHERLANDS 2
TÜRKIYE 1
ENGLAND 1
SWITZERLAND 1
ROMANIA 0
NETHERLANDS 3
AUSTRIA 1
TÜRKIYE 2
ENGLAND 2
SLOVAKIA 1
SWITZERLAND 2
ITALY 0

EURO 2024 TOP SCORERS				
		Goals	Assists	Games
1=	Dani Olmo	3	2	6
1=	Georges Mikautadze	3	1	4
1=	Cody Gakpo	3	1	6
1=	Ivan Schranz	3	0	4
1=	Jamal Musiala	3	0	5
1=	Harry Kane	3	0	7

TOP 5 PLAYERS

They say that there is no 'I' in team, but these 'i'ndividual players were at the top of their game this season, making their teams so much better. Is it time for a new name on the Ballon d'Or? These players certainly think so . . .

1 JUDE BELLINGHAM (REAL MADRID)

If you were going to write a football fairytale it'd look a lot like Bellingham's season.

Sign for the biggest team in the world? Tick
Score in each of his first four games? Tick
Win La Liga? Tick
Score 23 goals and assist 12? Tick
Receive La Liga Player of the Year award? Tick

And how would that football fairytale finish? With

the Champions League final . . . at Wembley . . . and against his former team, Borussia Dortmund.

The result? It was never in doubt . . .

A perfect blend of artist and warrior, 2023–24 was the season that Jude Bellingham confirmed that he is one of the best men's players in the world. Maybe even *the* best . . .

2 VINÍCIUS JÚNIOR (REAL MADRID)

'Ballon d'Or, no doubt,' said Real Madrid manager Carlo Ancelotti after Vinícius Junior's winner in the Champions League final. And while there's fierce competition (not least from his teammate Bellingham), Vinícius will have high hopes of being rewarded for another fantastic season.

The Brazilian winger is now the youngest player to score in two Champions League finals (beating Messi by 13 days). Contributing 27 goals over 40 matches for Los Blancos, Vinícius's confidence, flair and flamboyance bamboozled defenders all season.

The best in the world? Teammates Rodrygo, Lucas Vázquez and Bellingham all agree. So do legends Ronaldo Nazário, Thierry Henry and Rio Ferdinand. Who's to say they're wrong?

3 PHIL FODEN (MANCHESTER CITY)

While some players run, Foden glides. Since making his Manchester City debut, the young English talent has become more important with every season. And the 2023–24 season was his best yet.

With Kevin De Bruyne unavailable for long spells, Foden stepped up. His 25 goals and 11 assists were career bests. Whether playing as a winger or in the Number 10 role, he caused chaos in the penalty area with his fluid one-twos and sharp shooting. With hat-tricks against Brentford and Everton, along with important goals against Real Madrid and Manchester United, Foden was rewarded with the FWA Men's Footballer of the Year award.

4 KHADIJA 'BUNNY' SHAW (MANCHESTER CITY WOMEN)

Averaging a goal every sixty-six minutes, 'Bunny' Shaw fired Manchester City to within inches of the WSL title. If she'd remained fit for the final part of the season, who knows if City would have been able to claim their first title since 2016? Still, Shaw's 21 goals in 18 games were enough to win her the Golden Boot. And it wasn't just her goalscoring that impressed. She proved herself lethal in the air and strong as an ox when holding the ball up for her teammates. On the rare occasions when Manchester City didn't have the ball, she'd constantly use her intelligence to win the ball back.

5 AITANA BONMATÍ (FC BARCELONA FEMINÍ)

The current holder of the Ballon d'Or Féminin enjoyed another stellar season for Barcelona. Time and time again she stepped up to make the difference in big moments. Take the Champions League semi-final second leg against Chelsea, where she scored the first goal to level the tie on aggregate before winning the penalty which Fridolina Rolfo converted. Or the FOUR assists in ONE game against Levante. Or the game-changing display against Real Madrid. Or the opening goal in her player-of-the-match performance in the Champions League final.

The Spanish magician proved once again that she doesn't just play in games. She controls them. She has the trophies to back that up, as well as the stats (24 goals and 16 assists in 50 games).

ACTIVITIES

ANAGRAMS

These Ultimate Football Heroes have got all mixed up! Can you unscramble the anagrams to reveal their identities? All of them are featured in this book.

I Okay a Bauble ______________________

Mad Mole on Koala ______________________

Appeal By Mink ______________________

Iron Fir Waltz ______________________

Cancel Ride ______________________

Ah-ha, Jaws Kid! ______________________

A Manly Email ______________________

Jumbled Healing ______________________

Oh, Flip End ______________________

Jam Sale Menu ______________________

Natural Atomizer ______________________

Hm… Also Ahead ______________________

QUIZ TIME!

How much do you remember about the 2023–2024 season? Test your knowledge with this giant-sized quiz!

1 What was the score in the Community Shield that opened the Premier League season?

A. 1–0 to Arsenal

C. 3–2 to Arsenal

B. 1–0 to Manchester City

D. 4–1 to Manchester City

2 Wataru Endō plays for which Premier League team?

A. Arsenal

C. Newcastle

B. Chelsea

D. Liverpool

3 Who was the second-highest scorer in the Premier League, with 22 goals?

A. Ollie Watkins

B. Cole Palmer

C. Erling Haaland

D. Alexander Isak

4 How many times in a row have Manchester City won the league title?

A. 2

C. 4

B. 3

D. 5

5 How much did Saudi club Al-Ittihad reportedly offer for Mo Salah?

A. £75m

C. £125m

B. £100m

D. £150m

6 Which three teams were relegated to the Championship?

A. Everton, Burnley and Luton Town

B. Bournemouth, Burnley and Sheffield United

C. Luton Town, Nottingham Forest and Sheffield United

D. Burnley, Luton Town and Sheffield United

7 Which international team does Khadija 'Bunny' Shaw represent?

A. Jamaica

B. England

C. Trinidad and Tobago

D. USA

8 How many teams compete for the Women's Super League title?

A. 12

B. 14

C. 16

D. 18

9 Who came third in the WSL table behind Chelsea and Manchester City?

A. Tottenham

B. Arsenal

C. Manchester United

D. Liverpool

10 The team which knocked Chelsea out of the UEFA Women's Champions League went on to win the quadruple. Which team?

A. Ajax

B. Lyon

D. Barcelona

C. Paris St-Germain

11 Who won the WSL Golden Glove award for best goalkeeper of the season?

A. Mary Earps

B. Ellie Roebuck

C. Khiara Keating

D. Manuela Zinsberger

12 Who top-scored in the Champions League with 8 goals and 4 assists?

A. Harry Kane

B. Kylian Mbappé

C. Erling Haaland

D. Vinícius Júnior

13 Three of the four Real Madrid players with six Champions League medals are Toni Kroos, Luca Modrić, and Dani Carvajal. Who is the fourth?

A. Éder Militão

B. David Alaba

C. Nacho

D. Thibaut Courtois

14 Real Madrid's manager now has five Champions League medals. Who is he?

A. José Mourinho

B. Luiz Enrique

C. Carlo Ancelotti

D. Thomas Tuchel

15 How do you say 'the fifteenth' in Spanish?

A. *la decimoquinta*

B. *el quincuagésimo*

C. *la rinoceronte*

D. *el mediocampista*

16 Toni Kroos began his career in 2007 with which club?

A. Bayern Munich

B. Bayer Leverkusen

C. Leipzig

D. Borussia Dortmund

17 Ademola Lookman represents which international team?

A. Ghana

B. Nigeria

C. Senegal

D. Cameroon

18 18. Before winning the Europa League in 2023–24, how many European trophies had Atalanta won?

A. 0

B. 1

C. 2

D. 3

19 What are the home colours of Atalanta, in which they won the final?

A. Red with black stripes

B. Red with white stripes

C. Blue with black stripes

D. Blue with white stripes

20 Real Madrid's manager now has five Champions League medals. Who is he?

A. Pierre-Emerick Aubameyang

B. Ademola Lookman

C. Gianluca Scamacca

D. Florian Wirtz

21 Real Madrid's manager now has five Champions League medals. Who is he?

A. Nottingham Forest

B. Luton Town

C. Everton

D. Bournemouth

22 Which team did he accuse of being favoured by officials after a Premier League refereeing controversy?

A. Nottingham Forest

B. Luton Town

C. Everton

D. Bournemouth

23 What is the nickname of Inter Milan striker Lautaro Martínez?

A. *El conejo*

B. *El toro*

C. *El sapo*

D. *El delantero*

24 Which famous football stadium is the home of both Inter Milan and their bitter rivals AC Milan?

A. Stadio Olimpico

B. Stadio Renato Dall'Ara

C. Stadio delle Alpi

D. San Siro (Stadio Giuseppe Meazza)

25 What was remarkable about Lautaro's four goals against Salernitana?

A. All headers

B. He had come on as a substitute

C. All scored within the first half hour

D. Salernitana went on to win

26 How many times have Inter Milan now won the *Scudetto*?

A. 20

B. 21

C. 22

D. 23

27 Granit Xhaka, Bayer Leverkusen's Swiss midfielder, was bought from which Premier League team?

A. Arsenal

B. Tottenham Hotspur

C. Chelsea

D. Liverpool

28 How many years had Bayer Leverkusen gone without a Bundesliga trophy?

A. 40

B. 80

C. 120

D. 160

29 Leverkusen lost no games in the league. How many games did their nearest rivals lose?

A. 4

B. 5

C. 6

D. 7

30 Alex Grimaldo and Jeremie Frimpong excelled this season for Leverkusen in which position?

A. Central defence

B. Wing-back

C. Defensive midfield

D. Striker

31 With which two clubs had Leverkusen manager Xabi Alonso won the Champions League?

A. Manchester United and Real Madrid

B. Barcelona and Liverpool

C. Liverpool and Real Madrid

D. Bayern Munich and Barcelona

32 Who was the leading scorer in Spain with 24 goals?

A. Artem Dovbyk

B. Jude Bellingham

C. Vinícius Júnior

D. Robert Lewandowski

33 Which goalkeeper deputised for Thibaut Courtois during his injury spell?

A. Iñaki Peña

B. Horatiu Moldovan

C. Adrian

D. Andriy Lunin

34 How much was Jude Bellingham's transfer fee from Borussia Dortmund to Real Madrid?

A. £76.5 million

B. £88.5 million

C. £96.5 million

D. £108.5 million

35 *El Clasico* refers to any match between Real Madrid and which team?

A. Barcelona

B. Atletico Madrid

C. Real Sociedad

D. Valencia

36 How many times have Real Madrid won the La Liga title?

A. 33

B. 34

C. 35

D. 36

37 What is the name of Kylian Mbappé's younger brother, who made his senior debut for PSG in 2024?

A. Jirès

B. Wilfrid

C. Joseph

D. Ethan

38 Which team came second to PSG in Ligue 1?

A. Lyon

B. Monaco

C. Lens

D. Lille

39 Which team is Kylian Mbappé signing for on leaving PSG?

A. Real Madrid

B. Manchester City

C. Barcelona

D. AC Milan

40 Which of these is not a nickname for Celtic Football Club?

A. The Hoops

B. The Celts

C. The Bhoys

D. The Dons

41 Which Japanese striker scored 14 goals for Celtic?

A. Kyogo Furuhashi

B. Takuma Asano

C. Ayase Ueda

D. Daizen Maeda

42 How many teams compete in the Scottish Premier League?

A. 10

B. 12

C. 16

D. 20

43 Who was named man of the match in the final of Euro 2024?

A. Lamine Yamal

B. Cole Palmer

C. Mikel Merino

D. Nico Williams

44 What is the name given to the Euro 2024 trophy?

A. The Jules Rimet Trophy

B. The Henri Delaunay Cup

C. The Guillaume le Poisson Trophy

D. The Michel Platini Cup

45 Six players ended the tournament tied on goals scored. How many goals?

A. 3

B. 4

C. 5

D. 6

46 Which of the players from the previous question had the most assists?

A. Cody Gakpo

B. Harry Kane

C. Jamal Musiala

D. Dani Olmo

47 Who scored the equalising goal for England in the 73rd minute of the final?

A. Jude Bellingham

B. Cole Palmer

C. Harry Kane

D. Bukayo Saka

48 Who scored the winner in the Champions League final?

A. Rodrygo

B. Vinícius Júnior

C. Luka Modrić

D. Joselu

49 Which Premier League team beat Kylian Mbappé's PSG 4–1 in the Champions League group stage?

A. Arsenal

B. Liverpool

C. Newcastle United

D. Manchester City

50 Which Premier League team beat Kylian Mbappé's PSG 4–1 in the Champions League group stage?

A. Alejandro Garnacho

B. Marcus Rashford

C. Antony

D. Bruno Fernandes

LOGIC PROBLEM

Three friends, Anwar, Bill and Clare, have three seats together to watch England play at Euro 2024. Each supports a different Premier League team, and each is wearing a different England shirt – white, red, or the green goalkeeper jersey. Can you use the clues provided to work out who is wearing each shirt and who they support?

	Anwar	Bill	Clare	White	Red	Green
Arsenal						
Brighton						
Chelsea						
White						
Red						
Green						

Clues:

1. The Brighton fan is sitting directly to the left of the fan in the red shirt
2. There is one seat between the Brighton fan and the Chelsea fan
3. The person in the white shirt is directly to the right of the fan in the red shirt.

WORDSEARCH

The name of every single player who made it on to the pitch in the Euro 2024 final can be found in this wordsearch – all 29 of them! Can you find them in the grid running up, down, diagonally or backwards? When you have found them all the letters which remain unused will spell out a secret message. We've highlighted one to get you started!

N	O	M	I	S	I	A	N	U	K	C	O	Y	N	G
P	B	E	L	L	I	N	G	H	A	M	R	E	A	T
U	I	Z	C	A	I	L	A	A	N	A	C	N	T	I
Y	O	C	I	I	P	H	N	C	E	I	U	O	Z	S
A	T	O	K	U	R	O	E	S	H	N	C	T	U	P
M	O	A	S	F	R	I	R	U	N	O	U	A	B	N
A	L	D	D	N	O	N	B	T	G	O	R	S	I	R
L	M	E	E	N	I	R	A	T	E	T	E	M	M	E
R	O	D	R	I	A	K	D	I	E	R	L	A	E	K
M	O	R	A	T	A	M	T	L	B	W	L	I	N	L
F	U	L	A	J	A	V	R	A	C	A	A	L	D	A
S	E	N	O	T	S	C	K	O	W	H	F	L	I	W
L	A	B	A	Z	R	A	Y	O	N	S	K	I	N	E
X	T	T	I	M	S	P	A	L	M	E	R	W	E	T
O	E	O	N	I	R	E	M	N	G	L	L	A	N	D

CROSSWORD

This crossword contains all sorts of football-related terms. Can you crack the clues?

Across

1: Usually worn over the heart (5)
3: European football's governing body (4)
6: Everybody needs this for recovery (5)
7: The World Cup's governing body (4)
8: Another name for a bicycle? (7,4)
11: A team's main goal threat (7)
13: These help goalies handle the ball (6)
15: Warm-up weeks before the league starts (9)
16: International tournament won by Qatar in 2019 and 2023 (5,3)
18: Your team's lucky charm? (6)
20: Another half hour (5,4)
21: Borrow a player (4)
22: A cheeky pass behind you? (8)
23: Give a player time off to recover (4)

Down

1: Helps you stay on your feet (7)
2: The players at the back – and the offside trap (9,4)
4: Team supporters (4)
5: Giving the ball away is bad for this statistic (7,8)
6: Added for injuries (8,4)
9: This happens at least twice a game (7)
10: A player's uniform (3)
12: 2016, 2020 or 2024, perhaps? (4)
14: Watching teams or players to make sure you're prepared? (8)
15: A striker who snaps up chances – or a way to cook eggs? (7)
17: It must be at least 100 yards long and 50 yards wide (5)
19: A pass from the wing into the box (5)

MIXED UP CLUBS

Many English clubs have a suffix in their name. There are many familiar Cities, Uniteds and Towns, as well as unique ones like Stanley and Hotspur. Can you match all 20 of these suffixes to the right club?

Brighton & Hove	County
Crewe	Forest
Plymouth	Wednesday
Charlton	United
Stoke	Town
Derby	Albion
MK	Rangers
Nottingham	Villa
Tottenham	Rovers
Leyton	Moors
Preston	Alexandra
Queen's Park	Hotspur
Blackburn	North End
Accrington	City
Luton	Wanderers
Newcastle	Stanley
Aston	Dons
Bolton	Orient
Sheffield	Argyle
Solihull	Athletic

RIVALS

Football rivalries make the game even more exciting. Can you match up these teams with their most bitter rivals?

Barcelona	Galatasaray
Celtic	Everton
Boca Juniors	Borussia Dortmund
AC Milan	Real Madrid
Fenerbahçe	Palmeiras
Manchester United	Feyenoord
Liverpool	PSG
Bayern Munich	Porto
Newcastle	River Plate
Arsenal	Inter Milan
Ajax	Roma
Benfica	Rangers
Marseille	Manchester City
Lazio	Tottenham
Corinthians	Sunderland

DESIGN YOUR OWN KIT

What's your favourite football kit? Maybe it's the one your team plays in. Maybe you've always secretly admired the one your rivals play in. Or maybe it's a combination nobody's ever seen before…

Now's the chance to design your perfect kit. Plain? Stripes? Hoops? Patterns? Polka dots? It's up to you. We've even given you an extra blank kit so you can make an away strip!

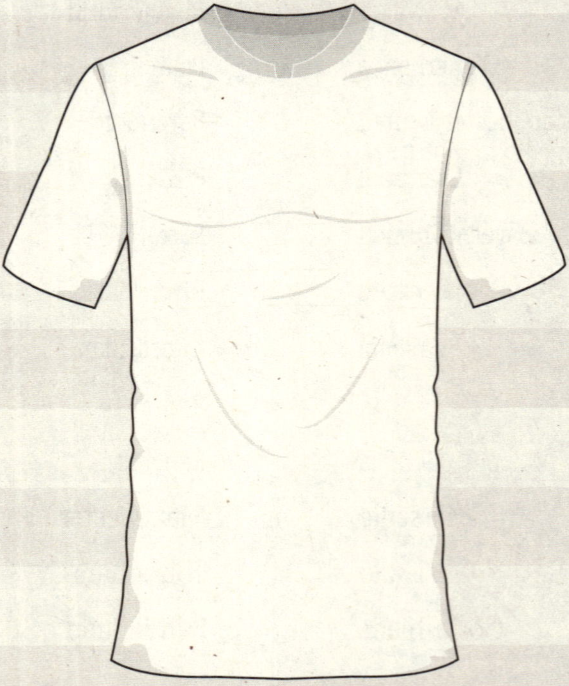

FOOTBALL BINGO

ACRES OF SPACE	WHAT'S THE REF GIVEN HERE	I'VE SEEN THEM GIVEN	IT'S A GAME OF TWO HALVES
ALMOST HIT THAT TOO WELL	THEY'VE PARKED THE BUS	IN AND AROUND THE PENALTY SPOT	THIS GAME NEEDS A GOAL
GOT TO HIT THE TARGET FROM THERE!	ANYWHERE WILL DO	THEY'LL BE OVER THE MOON	IF IT'S A YARD EITHER SIDE...
I FANCY THEM IN THE CUP THIS YEAR	A CRUNCHING TACKLE!	AT THE END OF THE DAY	IT'S A SIX-POINTER

Next time you're watching a match on the telly, play this game along with it. Whenever you hear a commentator use one of the footie phrases below, cross it off the bingo card. We've made two cards, so you can play against a friend. First one to fill up their card wins!

IF THAT'S ON TARGET, IT GOES IN	IT'S A SIX-POINTER	SOME TIRED LEGS OUT THERE	WHERE WAS THE MARKING?
THEY'LL BE OVER THE MOON	THEY'LL BE GUTTED ABOUT THAT	I FANCY THEM IN THE CUP THIS YEAR	A GOOD TIME TO SCORE
NO EASY GAMES AT THIS LEVEL	A WAKE-UP CALL	A NO-NONSENSE PLAYER	AT THIS LEVEL
NOBODY'S ON THE END OF IT	THEY'VE PARKED THE BUS	THEY'VE GOT TO SCORE THAT	HONOURS EVEN

ANSWERS

ANAGRAMS

I Okay a Bauble	Ayoub El Kaabi
Mad Mole on Koala	Ademola Lookman
Appeal By Mink	Kylian Mbappé
Iron Fir Waltz	Florian Wirtz
Cancel Ride	Declan Rice
Ah-ha, Jaws Kid!	Khadija Shaw
A Manly Email	Lamine Yamal
Jumbled Healing	Jude Bellingham
Oh, Flip End	Phil Foden
Jam Sale Menu	Lauren James
Natural Atomizer	Lautaro Martinez
Hm… Also Ahead	Mohamed Salah

QUIZ

1) A, 2) D, 3) B, 4) C, 5) C, 6) D, 7) A, 8) A, 9) B, 10) D, 11) C, 12) A, 13) C, 14) C, 15) A, 16) A, 17) B, 18) B, 19) C, 20) A, 21) A, 22) B, 23) B, 24) D, 25) B, 26) A, 27) A, 28) C, 29) D, 30) B, 31) C, 32) A, 33) D, 34) B, 35) A, 36) D, 37) D, 38) B, 39) A, 40) D, 41) A, 42) B, 43) D, 44) B, 45) A, 46) D, 47) B, 48) B, 49) C, 50) A

LOGIC PROBLEM

Anwar supports Brighton and is wearing the green jersey; Bill is an Arsenal fan and is wearing red; Clare is a Chelsea fan and is wearing white.

CROSSWORD

ACROSS: 1) Badge, 3) UEFA, 6) Sleep, 7) FIFA, 8) Scissor kick, 11) Striker, 13) Gloves, 15) Preseason, 16) Asian Cup, 18) Mascot, 20) Extra time, 21) Loan, 22) Backheel, 23) Rest

DOWN: 1) Balance, 2) Defensive line, 4) Fans, 5) Passing accuracy, 6) Stoppage time, 9) Kickoff, 10) Kit, 12) Euro, 14) Scouting, 15) Poacher, 17) Pitch, 19) Cross

WORDSEARCH

N	O	M	I	S	I	A	N	U	K	C	O	Y	N	G
P	B	E	L	L	I	N	G	H	A	M	R	E	A	T
U	I	Z	C	A	I	L	A	A	N	A	C	N	T	I
Y	O	C	I	I	P	H	N	C	E	I	U	O	Z	S
A	T	O	K	U	R	O	E	S	H	N	C	T	U	P
M	O	A	S	F	R	I	R	U	N	O	U	A	B	N
A	L	D	D	N	O	N	B	T	G	O	R	S	I	R
L	M	E	E	N	I	R	A	T	E	T	E	M	M	E
R	O	D	R	I	A	K	D	I	E	R	L	A	E	K
M	O	R	A	T	A	M	T	L	B	W	L	I	N	L
F	U	L	A	J	A	V	R	A	C	A	A	L	D	A
S	E	N	O	T	S	C	K	O	W	H	F	L	I	W
L	A	B	A	Z	R	A	Y	O	N	S	K	I	N	E
X	T	T	I	M	S	P	A	L	M	E	R	W	E	T
O	E	O	N	I	R	E	M	N	G	L	L	A	N	D

MIXED-UP CLUBS

Brighton & Hove Albion, Crewe Alexandra, Plymouth Argyle, Charlton Athletic, Stoke City, Derby County, MK Dons, Nottingham Forest, Tottenham Hotspur, Leyton Orient, Preston North End, Queen's Park Rangers, Blackburn Rovers, Accrington Stanley, Luton Town, Newcastle United, Aston Villa, Bolton Wanderers, Sheffield Wednesday

RIVALS

Barcelona and Real Madrid; Celtic and Rangers; Boca Juniors and River Plate; AC Milan and Inter Milan; Fenerbahçe and Galatasaray; Manchester United and Manchester City; Liverpool and Everton; Bayern Munich and Borussia Dortmund; Newcastle and Sunderland; Arsenal and Tottenham; Ajax and Feyenoord; Benfica and Porto; Marseille and PSG; Lazio and Roma; Corinthians and Palmeiras